Sailing Home

A Katama Bay Series

Katie Winters

ALL RIGHTS RESERVED. No part of this publication may be reproduced, distributed, or transmitted in any form or by any means, including photocopying, recording, or other electronic or mechanical methods, without the prior written permission of the publisher.

Copyright © 2023 by Katie Winters

This is a work of fiction. Any resemblance of characters to actual persons, living or dead is purely coincidental. Katie Winters holds exclusive rights to this work. Unauthorized duplication is prohibited.

Chapter One

The British Virgin Islands

It was the seagulls that awoke her. Long shadows dipped across the top window of her sailboat as the birds flocked overhead, squawking to bring in the new day. It was the first day of the British Virgin Islands Regatta, and in the early light of that morning, Whitney Silverton felt wide open to the possibility of winning. None of the other sailors across the Caribbean could hold a candle to her. And they knew it.

Whitney stretched her long legs so that her toes dug into the far end of the berth, the area below the deck of her sailboat that contained a mattress, a small shelf for her personal things, and not much else. What else could she possibly need? She had the world's oceans at her feet.

Across the harbor outside of Parham Town, the other sailors who'd slept aboard their sailboats began to greet one another. Whitney lifted her head from the berth and peered across the glittering turquoise of the water. Two docks away, a sailor she vaguely recognized hovered over the side of his boat, brushing his teeth. As he shook his arm from side to side, his white beard shook along with him. Other sailors across the harbor began to boil hot water for instant coffee, scratching their appendages and waving hello.

Whitney, one of the only women who slept alone across the harbor, leaped to the deck and instinctively checked the ropes that tethered her to the dock. It was something her father had taught her: *always double-check. Better safe than sorry.*

He'd also taught her a fair number of sailing superstitions: *never re-name your boat, don't trust flat-footed people on board, and naturally, that women were bad luck at sea.* Her father had always laughed at that one. "Let the sea be angry," he'd said. "You belong out here. With me."

"Morning, Whit!" A sailor named Gregory waved an arm from two boats over. He was a Scottish-born sailor who'd spent a great deal of his days at sea and a great deal of his nights deep inside a bottle of rum. Whitney suspected he'd left someone behind in Scotland. Loneliness lurked in his eyes.

"Hi, Greg!" Whitney called back. "How'd the night treat you?"

"Afraid I'm none too fresh for the race today," Gregory told her as he palmed his neck.

"You'll find a way to pull yourself together," Whitney teased. "You always do."

"We're not all Whitney Silverton," Gregory reminded her, rubbing his beer belly as he gazed out across the water. "My God, look at this morning. It's spectacular, isn't it?"

Sailing Home

Whitney had awoken to thousands of similar mornings across the Caribbean. She often had to pinch herself to acknowledge the glorious nature of every brand-new day. Her father had said, "It's a curse that we live in paradise. We can't possibly remember what we have."

Whitney boiled a pot of water and poured nuggets of instant coffee into a mug that read HAPPY FATHER'S DAY, which she'd bought for her dad thirty-five years ago with money she'd earned aboard another man's ship. Her dad had accidentally left the mug back in the Caribbean after he'd moved. She'd kept it to honor her excitement when she'd first bought it for him. Finally, she'd thought, she could give her best friend in the world a gift to show just how much he meant to her.

Whitney perched at the edge of her sailboat, her steaming mug beside her as she scrolled through her smartphone. Like many others in the sailing community, she'd avoided getting a smartphone until the last possible moment— but now found herself occasionally checking weather patterns, sailing community updates, and what her godforsaken ex-boyfriend had posted lately. No, it wasn't healthy to check on Garrett. But "healthy" wasn't exactly Whitney Silverton's middle name.

She had to believe that everyone had their vices. Hers involved assessing whether Garrett and his new girlfriend had called it quits.

It wasn't that she wanted to get back with him. No. Her heart still ached with the memory of what they'd once been— the most renowned couple in the sailing community, recognized from coast to coast and harbor to harbor. For ten years, they'd been blissfully in love and had often taken off for the wild seas, making love in the berth and then arising for the most gorgeous of days. Time felt different out at sea. You only knew the water, the sun, and the wind. You fell into nature completely.

Unfortunately, Garrett hadn't updated any of his social media profiles in six weeks. The last photo, which had been burned into Whitney's mind, featured him aboard the sailboat they'd picked out together. He held a fish above his head and smiled that arrogant smile of his. If only he weren't so handsome. If only he hadn't broken her heart.

The Regatta began at noon. It was only seven thirty, and Whitney felt the hours stretch out before her, making her anxious. She had to do something to take the edge off. She moved into the berth and staggered into a pair of running shorts, then scooped herself into a sports bra. In three minutes, she found herself back on land, pounding into a run as her earphones blasted an upbeat song. It was cheesy, but "Eye of the Tiger" almost always put her in the mood to win.

She ran east along East End Bay, curving along the coastline until she reached the bridge that led to Beef Island. How she'd adored the name "Beef Island" as a kid. She'd howled to her dad, "Come on! Let's sail to Beef Island!" and then fallen to the ground, giggling until a stitch ran up her side.

Before the bridge, Whitney staggered to a halt and gasped for breath. She stretched out her muscular legs, which now featured a whole lot more cellulite than she was fully comfortable with. At forty-three years old, Whitney faced the second half of her life. *Would she do it all alone?*

It was difficult not to remind herself that Garrett's new girlfriend seemed not to have a hint of cellulite. She

Sailing Home

wasn't a sailor, had an actual apartment with a big refrigerator (according to photos Whitney had seen online), and seemed to brush and style her hair every single day. If that was what Garrett wanted, Whitney had to be okay with that. Somehow.

Whitney took this opportunity to drop her dark-red hair from its familiar ponytail and fluff it out. She then dabbed the sweat from her forehead and cheeks, took a deep breath, and finally willed herself to call her dad on video chat. Despite the circumstances, she still adored seeing his face.

Tyson Silverton answered the call, appearing before her in his ratty British Virgin Island's Regatta T-shirt from 1987.

"There she is! My sweet girl!"

Whitney's heart lifted. "Hi, Dad! Guess where I am?"

Her father pretended to search the small area behind her head. "You'll have to give me a hint."

"I'm right by Beef Island!" Whitney said, flashing the phone toward the bridge.

"Wow! There it is. Hard to believe I haven't seen the British Virgin Islands in over ten years," Tyson replied, shaking his head.

"They're right here, waiting for you," Whitney said, flashing him an infectious smile.

"Maybe I can make it there before the race," Tyson said. "Someone needs to get down there and show you real sailing."

Whitney cackled. "You taught me everything I know."

"That's why you're bound to win today," he told her.

"I have a feeling. And you know how powerful my feelings are."

"Right. I see someone has a selective memory," Whitney teased. "I seem to remember someone having a 'feeling' that the weather wouldn't turn, which led us to get caught in a tropical storm."

"You know the sea was angry that day," Tyson joked. "A woman out at sea! Unthinkable."

Whitney stuck out her tongue playfully, and Tyson mirrored her right back.

"Grow up, Dad," Whitney quipped.

"If only I could," Tyson replied wistfully.

Whitney's smile widened. For a beautiful moment, she allowed herself to believe in miracles. But only a split second later, Tyson's face crumpled as he burst into another round of coughing. The coughing was so powerful that it made his shoulders shake and tears spill from his eyes.

A lung cancer diagnosis had come three years ago.

The doctor said he didn't have much time left. Then again, the doctor had said that for the last three years. Tyson's longevity was due to his stubbornness, Whitney knew. Nothing and nobody brought down Tyson Silverton— not the wild waves out at sea, punch-happy sailors, or lung cancer itself.

"Ah, sorry," Tyson managed as the last coughs petered out. "Haven't drunk enough water this morning."

He always made an excuse like that. Anything that allowed them both to believe that his coughing was just run-of-the-mill, something that happened to everyone.

"You have to stay hydrated," Whitney told her father dutifully.

Sailing Home

"Will do. Liz keeps me in check, anyway," Tyson said, adjusting the collar of his T-shirt.

Liz was Tyson's first and only wife, a woman he'd married during Whitney's late twenties. Like Garrett's new girlfriend, Liz was a non-sailor, a woman who understood the appeal of staying in one place for a little while. When Whitney had visited their home in Miami, Florida, she'd been amazed at how well-stocked the pantry was. "Dad, you have four types of chips," she'd told him. To this, Tyson had just shrugged. "We do bulk grocery shopping on Sundays."

Whitney and Tyson had shopped when they'd needed to, lived off crap when they'd wanted to, and generally never bothered to plan ahead longer than a couple of days. That era was over with, at least for Tyson.

"Hey, honey. I have to run," Tyson said. His eyes watered as though he sensed another coughing fit coming along. "Promise me you'll win today."

"Talk about pressure," Whitney shot back, smiling.

"You can handle pressure," Tyson explained. "That's always been a talent of yours. All the other sailors across the Caribbean couldn't believe how capable you were at such a young age. I just shrugged and said, 'It's all her.'"

Whitney's heart ballooned. "I love you, Dad."

"I love you, too. But I'll love you more if you win that Regatta today."

"Dad!" Whitney howled.

"I'm just trying to be honest," Tyson said mischievously.

After Whitney and Tyson hung up, Whitney crumpled to a heap on the boardwalk and allowed herself to cry for a full two minutes. It wasn't a soft, subtle cry; it was the kind of cry that made her body quake and her shoulders tip toward her ears. The animalistic noises that came from her throat didn't sound like her at all.

After about two minutes, she forced herself to her feet, directed herself back toward the harbor, and began lifting her knees into a run.

Her father had demanded a win from her that day. And she wasn't the sort of daughter to let him down.

Chapter Two

The British Virgin Islands' most populated town, Road Town, was still nothing more than a little village. As the residents awoke that Saturday morning at the start of September, Cole Steel walked out of the Road Town Bakery, holding a large paper bag of baked goods under his arm. At that point, he'd been in the Caribbean for nearly two months, spending multiple days out on the water, building muscle, darkening his tan, and growing accustomed to the slow and peaceful way of life all the way down south. It wasn't Martha's Vineyard—nothing was—but he still imagined he could get used to it, despite the ache in his gut that told him just how homesick he was.

The apartment was just a rental, a reprieve from his long nights sleeping in the berth of any given sailboat. As he opened the door, the other temporary residents of the rental apartment greeted him excitedly from the kitchen.

"Cole!"

Elsa Remington Steel popped from the kitchen with a glass of orange juice lifted. She hadn't yet done her makeup, but she was tanned and beautiful in the soft light of the morning. "I just can't get over seeing your face!" she said as she took the bag of baked goods and tapped his cheek.

"Mom, come on." Cole rolled his eyes, teasing her.

Cole's sister Mallory sat in a pair of overalls and a swimsuit top in the kitchen, sipping juice. Beside her, her toddler, Zachery, whacked his plastic spoon across a high chair and greeted his uncle Cole with a squawk.

"There he is. My main man!" Cole said, greeting Zachery.

Alexie, Cole's youngest sister, popped out from the side bedroom, rubbing her fists over her eyes. Over the summer, she'd dyed her hair a horrific shade of pink, but it had slowly grown out so that only the edges looked dried out and rose-colored.

"Did you get croissants?" Alexie demanded.

Elsa ruffled the paper bag, inspecting the bakery items. "He pulled through for us. I see regular croissants, chocolate croissants, a few éclairs, and some classic rolls."

"Thank goodness. I'm starving." Alexie dropped into another chair around the kitchen table. Often, Cole couldn't help but think that Alexie had turned into the true "brat" of the family. Her move to New York City to attend art school had only exacerbated the problem. The rest of the family ignored her.

Mallory's eyes glittered knowingly. "Are you nervous?"

Cole grimaced. "No? I don't know. Maybe?"

Elsa handed him a steaming mug of coffee. "You're going to be great out there."

"I don't know. The Caribbean has a different league

of sailors altogether," Cole explained, grabbing a croissant and heading to the table.

"Yes, and you're one of them, now," Elsa reminded him, her hand on her hip. "Although in my heart, you'll always be a Martha's Vineyard islander, through and through."

"Mine, too," Mallory added with a wink.

Cole sipped his coffee contemplatively, trying to ignore the anxiety that wiggled through his stomach. In only a few hours, he would face the other competitors in the British Virgin Islands Regatta, rushing out across the waves of a far different ocean than he was used to. He'd come to the Caribbean to race competitively, work alongside lifelong sailors, and make money in the sailing industry. This was all a part of his elaborate plan.

The reality just wasn't as easy as dreaming about it.

Another door within the rental apartment creaked open. A few seconds later, Bruce Holland appeared in the doorway, his smile strained. This was his first vacation with the Steel family, and it was clear to all of them, including Bruce, that Aiden Steel should have been there instead.

Cole's father had died several years ago at that point. Despite Cole's most shameful wishes, Elsa had met Bruce Holland the previous year, fallen in love, and recently gotten engaged. It wasn't that Cole didn't like Bruce; in fact, Bruce was an upstanding man with a great career, a kind family, and a similar sorrowful past. That said, Bruce would never take Aiden's place. It was plain and simple.

"Morning!" Bruce hollered a little too loudly.

"Good morning, honey." Elsa stepped over to kiss Bruce on the cheek. Cole looked away. "How was your run?"

Bruce shook his head. "The humidity almost killed me. I don't know how you deal with it, Cole."

Cole waved a hand. He could have told Bruce that he'd soaked through several T-shirts during his first few days in the Caribbean, but he decided against it.

"You get used to it," he said instead.

"I should hope so," Bruce affirmed. "The shower hardly cooled me down at all."

Elsa and Mallory cooked scrambled eggs and sausages while another pot of coffee bubbled and spat. Cole's anxiety about the approaching race caused him to pace from the kitchen to the balcony and back again. Alexie filed her nails as Bruce played a word game on his phone. In the meantime, Zachery had begun to fade, his eyelids drooping toward his cheeks.

"Look at him," Mallory cooed. "He's starting to regret that he got his mama up at five in the morning." She lifted him from his high chair and prepared to put him back to sleep. Very soon, the entire family would head out to get a good spot for the Regatta celebration, with the hopes to see Cole glide across the finish line first.

Elsa scooped several dollops of scrambled eggs onto a large plate. She then lined the plate with greasy sausages and placed it in front of an empty chair. "Cole! Breakfast!"

Cole was ravenous. His life out to sea didn't often allow him such decadent breakfasts. As he ate, he remembered the previous week, when he'd helped another sailor charter a cruise for tourists through the British and United States Virgin Islands. They hadn't prepared enough food for all the guests, and Cole had been forced to sustain himself on protein bars and peanuts.

Together, the Steel family and Bruce Holland ate as

Sailing Home

the winds rushed from the bay through the open windows. Alexie ate sparingly, nibbling at the edge of a sausage. Cole imagined the city had taught her that, too.

Mallory chatted easily about her newfound "legal" life on Martha's Vineyard, where she'd continued to intern for Bruce and Susan Sheridan at the Sheridan Law Office in Oak Bluffs. On top of that, she'd begun online courses with the hope of someday attending law school. Cole was genuinely impressed with his sister for taking that leap so late in life— after a failed engagement and a child. He liked to think of it as proof that you could change your mind about your life whenever you wanted. The rules were up to you.

"She has a killer instinct," Bruce said, mostly eyeing Cole. "And a truly spectacular memory. When you tell her something, she sucks it in like a sponge."

After Cole scraped his plate clean, he changed his clothes and hugged his mother goodbye. Elsa squeezed him extra hard and whispered, "Your father is watching you today. I hope you know that."

Cole often felt his father's presence out on the water. He could hear his voice, reminding him of tasks to perform and the different ways to shift the sails. Often, he returned from solo sails bleary-eyed, as it felt as though Cole and Aiden had been out at sea together— rushing out across the waters and leaving the sorrows of life behind.

Bruce raised a hand to high-five Cole. Cole smacked his hand, feeling foolish.

"Go get 'em," Bruce said, palming the back of his neck.

"Thanks," Cole returned, his voice low.

Would the two of them have any kind of friendship in the future? Cole couldn't say.

"Good luck, big brother!" Alexie called.

"Go show them what you're all about!" Mallory added.

Cole headed to the port, where he'd tethered the sailboat that he planned to use for the race. Around him, Road Town flourished, with islanders already in the beginning stages of celebrating the Regatta ahead. Caribbean residents knew the ins and outs of parties; they saw no issues in quitting work by three and enjoying the rest of the day. Their smiles widened as Cole passed, and several people greeted him, calling out, "Good luck to you, sir!" Cole knew that he now looked the part of a sailor. The broad shoulders, the tan, and the swagger gave it away. He waved a hand back, thanking them. He would need all the help he could get.

Down at the harbor, the sailors participating in the Regatta paced every which way across the docks. Their conversations roared above the boats and stretched out across the water, becoming a thick cloud of sound. A few of the Caribbean sailors clapped Cole on the back as he headed for his boat, wishing him well.

"He's got that fresh-faced enthusiasm," an older sailor with a white beard croaked as Cole passed. "I remember having that. I thought nobody could defeat me."

Often, Cole grew anxious about the fact that these sailors seemed cut from a different cloth than he was. Despite his sailing roots, he'd grown up in a loving home on Martha's Vineyard. He'd attended all of high school, had adored both his mother and father, had participated in local Martha's Vineyard community events, and had

Sailing Home

taught his little sisters what he could about how to survive.

The sailors in the Caribbean, however, were salt of the earth. Often, they'd lost a father or a mother or hadn't known either of them at all. Some had been raised on the open seas and therefore had no sense of stability. To them, the idea of staying in one place for a little while was akin to being in prison.

Cole, who'd hardly stayed in one harbor for longer than a night or two since July, ached to have a more permanent address. He questioned that instinct, knowing that it wasn't what you were meant to have in the sailing world. Still, it remained like a seed growing in his stomach.

Several boats over from his own, the renowned female sailor, Whitney Silverton, made last-minute adjustments on her gorgeous vessel. Her red hair whipped wildly in the wind, and her tanned and muscular arms worked diligently. Whitney was much like the other sailors you met across the Caribbean in that she'd hardly ever learned the concept of home, had probably sailed most places across the earth, and had never been married or had children. That said, she was also a darn good sailor, often deemed the best of the best. She intimidated many sailors, perhaps because of what she represented: that men didn't always have the power.

In fact, based on what Cole knew of his mother, his aunt Carmella, his stepgrandmother Nancy, and his stepaunt Janine, he felt that women often held most of the power— yet knew how to wield it in ways men didn't. He could only respect that.

"Hey, mate." An English sailor caught Cole's attention on the boat between his and Whitney's. "Good luck out there, yeah?"

"Good luck to you," Cole returned, shaking out of his reverie. "We're going to need it."

"Especially racing alongside her." The English sailor tipped his head back toward Whitney. "I get all shaky when I see her prepping up. I know she knows something about the water that I don't."

Cole laughed, although his guts twisted with fear. "I have a hunch that she'll never tell us what she knows."

"Right you are, my lad," the English sailor replied, shaking his head. "Right you are."

Chapter Three

Whitney yanked the rope from the dock, wrapping its scratchy, wet material around and around her elbow as the boat creaked out from land. Her heart thumped in her chest as she eased past other racers, all headed for the starting line and prepared to head out to open seas. A few boats over, her father's friend, a sailor named Randy, lifted a hand in greeting. Whitney just nodded in return. Now wasn't the time for pleasantries. Now was the time to win.

A woman in a red bikini and a sash that read MISS ROAD TOWN stood out on a pier with a big red flag lifted. Her smile was frozen, like concrete across her cheeks. As a girl, Whitney had marveled at women like her— women who upheld their beauty over all things. As far as Whitney could tell, especially after sailing around the world, beauty was something that disappeared quickly. *What were you left with when it disappeared?* She wasn't sure. She supposed she'd learn sooner rather than later.

The air was taut with tension. Every sailor tilted

forward, watching that bright red flag as it fluttered in the Caribbean breeze. If Whitney shifted her perception just so, she could imagine her father a few boats over, prepared to race. Back in her twenties, they'd only raced one another a handful of times and had preferred, instead, to race as a team. Each time they'd raced, Tyson had beaten her without issue. She'd learned so much from her father and had gotten far better since then.

A man with a megaphone stood alongside the woman in the bikini on the pier. He wore a big blue baseball hat that read BVI REGATTA 2022. Whitney's heart surged with love for her father, who'd worn his 1987 British Virgin Islands Regatta T-shirt in honor of her race.

"Sailors, on your mark. Get set. GO!"

As the "go" rang out, the woman in the bikini flashed the flag down like a sword. Everyone burst forward, gliding across the turquoise waters to gain an early first lead. Just as ever, Whitney's initial pre-race jitters were replaced with excitement. She now felt cool and calculated, as though time slowed itself to a halt and allowed her to anticipate other sailors' decisions, gliding in and out of their wake as she made her way to the front.

It didn't take long before she found herself a full ten feet in front of the second-place position. Her sail ballooned out in front of her, pushing her forward, and the water beneath her was like glass. Everything seemed easy and simple. She found space to breathe again.

Unfortunately, this space allowed other thoughts to grow. These thoughts had everything to do with the harsh reality of her life and little to do with the race at hand.

Her father. The strong and powerful Tyson Silverton. As a girl, Whitney had thought of him as a superhero or a magician; the sailboat beneath them had been a sort of

Sailing Home

magic carpet, gliding them across the earth. Wherever they'd wanted to go, the boat had taken them there.

Whitney's education had been the water, the wind, and the sun— nothing more. Only twice that Whitney could remember, someone had asked about Whitney's "actual" education. Some of the sailors' children remained at home with the wives or girlfriends, attending school from Monday to Friday. Because Whitney's mother had left Whitney when she was no more than five months old, Whitney had nowhere to stay and nowhere to go. Tyson Silverton had no plans to stay on land, just for little Whitney to learn a little "two plus two." He would teach her everything.

And eventually, he had gotten around to filing the paperwork that declared her officially homeschooled. Eventually was better than never.

Someone hollered across the water, snapping Whitney from her reverie. She turned to find another sailboat surging toward her. She'd lost track of herself, falling into the depths of her memories. She couldn't let her own nostalgia ruin her chance at the race.

Whitney forced herself to focus on the sails, the tautness of the rope, the whipping winds, and the coastline to her side, which allowed her to keep track of the racecourse. "Come on, Whitney," she muttered to herself.

With her brain and body back in gear, the boat faded back toward the others. Whitney dared herself to glance back and take in the sight of over fifty sailboats headed toward her. It was funny to imagine them as a pirate troupe chasing after her. This, too, she had learned from her father— never trust anyone at sea.

Everyone was out to get you. Everyone wanted to take you for all you had.

Very soon, however, she grew lost in her thoughts that had everything to do with her father and her life regrets and nothing at all to do with the race.

She discovered herself growing especially resentful of that time in her twenties when she'd cultivated a group of sailing friends and roamed the waters alone. When she'd finally met back up with her father on the British Virgin Islands, he'd introduced her to his brand-new (and very first in decades) girlfriend, Liz.

Whitney never should have abandoned him like that. He'd fallen in love and built a life back in Miami, where Liz had grown up. Despite their gorgeous past, Tyson Silverton had moved on to the next era.

It happened again. Whitney's thoughts clouded her mind, and very soon, a number of other sailboats licked her boots. She made the mistake of glancing back a little too far and nearly lost her balance on deck but then tugged herself back up with the same rope she used for the sails. The sails tilted slightly and plotted her off course for a moment.

"Novice," she told herself angrily. "What makes you think these people can't beat you? Because if you let them, they will."

One of the sailboats that eased closer and closer had a younger man at the ropes, his eyes wide open and optimistic as he surged forward. Based on a cursory glance, he seemed like a damn good sailor, the kind that had been born with the instincts that others had to learn. If Whitney had to guess, he looked to be in his mid-to-late twenties, and he was less rugged than the others. Probably, he hadn't had the ragtag lifestyle of many sailors— although, if he was in the Caribbean, it wouldn't be long till he looked just as rough.

Sailing Home

Living the way they did could take a toll on you. Whitney sustained herself with a healthy diet, some running, less alcohol (certainly far less than in her twenties), and decent nights of sleep, which meant she didn't wear the trauma of sea life as much as others. Still, sometimes the loneliness ate her up.

The race wore on. Whitney continued to shove away thoughts of her pain, gliding forward just a hair ahead of the younger sailor and several of the others, many of whom she'd raced several times throughout her career. Sometimes, those guys managed to beat her, which always put gloating smiles on their faces. She hated those smiles. She would do anything not to see them that day.

By the time the sailors spotted the finish line, the crowd along the harbor had grown five times as dense. Revelers waited expectantly to cheer on the sailors during the last stretch, their pints of beers lifted and their noses shiny red from the sun.

Whitney used the crowd to dig deep within herself for the courage to finish first. She knew that among non-sailors, she was something of a favorite. She couldn't let down her fans, least of all the little girls who looked up to her and dreamed of a future where they could do that, too.

The last stretch wasn't easy. The wind tore through Whitney's red hair and scratched her cheeks and lips with salt. Her stomach groaned with hunger, and her taut muscles bordered on exhaustion.

The same woman in a red bikini stood out on the pier with the flag lifted. Another man crouched down, prepared to take several photographs for sailing publications across the world. Whitney forced her eyes forward, telling herself to remember this moment.

As she crossed over the finish line split seconds before the others in the race, her heart lifted toward the sky, and she felt weightless, invincible. This was why she did it. This moment, with the crowd wailing and crying her name, was better than anything else.

She'd won, just as she'd told her father she would.

Whitney pounded her fist through the air as the crowd screamed louder. On either side of her, the second, third, and fourth place finishers glided back toward the docks, coming close enough to high-five and congratulate one another. One of the men met Whitney's gaze and nodded, his eyes shadowed with embarrassment.

Yet again, they were ashamed that they'd been beaten by a woman.

Only the younger sailor raised a hand from two boats over and shouted, "Congratulations!" His smile was genuine, open, and contagious.

Whitney wanted to scream back, *Who the heck are you?* But instead, she remained demure and waved back, saying, "Thank you. Good race."

Back at the docks, Whitney tied up her boat tightly and collapsed at the edge of the stern. She drank the entirety of her water bottle, then undressed down to her swimsuit and dove into the water's blue depths. Below the surface, her thoughts slowed, and her ears pounded.

Far, far away, her father was dying of lung cancer in Liz's bed. It was surreal at best and felt like a slow squeeze around her heart.

Back on the deck, Whitney closed her fists over her long hair and shot out of the water. The sailors who'd tied up around her continued to high-five and crack open bottles of beer. The tension preceding the race had disappeared, allowing an air of celebration and relief. They'd done it; they'd really done it.

Down the dock, a crowd of people surrounded the younger sailor. Two women in their twenties, one with a baby, a woman in her mid-to-late forties, and an anxious-looking man stood around him, wearing broad smiles. The forty-something woman flailed forward and hugged the sailor as the sailor's cheeks turned crimson.

Ah, Whitney laughed to herself. She'd been right. This young man wasn't like the other sailors in the area. He had loved ones who came to his race and cheered him on as if their lives depended on it. Whitney wanted to shake him for his embarrassment. He had no idea what he had.

Whitney grabbed a black dress, flipped it over her swimsuit, and headed down the dock to say hello. This sailor could have beaten her. But when she'd pulled it out, he'd waved across the water to her, just grateful to be next in line.

As Whitney approached, she caught some of what the family around the young sailor said.

The forty-something woman said, "Cole, you looked just like your father as you crossed the finish line. He always smiled like that, as though he'd learned a secret along the race route."

Cole's cheeks burned even brighter, even as his beautiful blue eyes glinted joyously. Beside the forty-something woman, a young woman with pink-tinged hair said, "I had no idea that you would manage to be in the top ten, let alone the top five."

"Gee. Thanks for believing in me," Cole shot back.

The toddler in the other young woman's arms raised

an arm and swatted Cole playfully. Cole brought his arms around him as the little boy cried, "Unc-a Co!"

Whitney's heart surged with emotion. Probably, it was just adrenaline from the race. She forced herself forward. All she had to do was say hello.

"Cole, right?" She appeared beside him wearing what she hoped was a genuine smile.

Cole's eyes widened with surprise. The toddler in his arms squawked his hello.

"Ms. Silverton!" he said. "Congratulations. It was such an honor to race with you today."

Ms. Silverton! She'd never been called that. What kind of manners did this boy have? Did he know they wouldn't fly in the sailing community? Whitney glanced toward his family, who peered at her curiously. Maybe it was clear to them that she'd hardly ever eaten a home-cooked dinner.

"Right back atcha," Whitney returned. She then spoke to who she assumed was his mother, saying, "Cole has real potential. I felt him creeping up behind me and knew I had to kick in gear."

The woman grinned madly. "We think he's pretty talented, but we're biased."

Whitney laughed good-naturedly and sauntered around the family, pretending she was on her way someplace else. "Looking forward to seeing your future career, Cole," Whitney added, dropping her chin with respect. "Enjoy the rest of the day with your family."

And with that, she headed off the dock to no place in particular. The Regatta Awards wouldn't begin for another two hours. Maybe she would grab a beer in the shade before then and try to pretend she didn't feel so alone.

Chapter Four

The British Virgin Islands Regatta First Place Award caught the last light of the evening. It sat on the slanted window of Whitney's berth next to several other awards and honors. Already, Whitney set her sights on the next time she needed to prove herself worthy of her name.

Whitney tugged a pair of jean shorts over her hips and donned a black tank top. With the mirror that hung on the berth door, she slid golden hoops through her ears, smeared lipstick on her lips, and even added a hint of mascara. When she stepped back, she took in a vision of herself as a "woman." It was a rare thing to see herself in this way, especially since Garrett had left. Still, she welcomed it.

Before Whitney headed out for the sailing party along the harbor, she tried again to call her father. She ached to tell him about her big win. After the third ring, however, a female's voice answered.

"Whitney? You're going to need to try him tomorrow."

Whitney's heart dropped into her stomach. "Oh. Hi, Liz." She hated that Liz hadn't even given her stepdaughter a simple "hello."

"He's fast asleep," Liz told her. "He hardly got a wink last night due to all the coughing."

"Okay. Yeah." Whitney wondered if she could trust Liz to pass along the news of the race to her father. Given that Liz didn't give two hoots about sailing, she imagined it wasn't a great idea. "I'll give him a call tomorrow."

"All right. Take care—"

"Wait. Liz?" Whitney staggered up from the berth and into the pinkish light of the evening. "How is he doing? I mean, besides the lack of sleep and the coughing."

Liz heaved a sigh directly through the speaker. Whitney could feel the woman's exhaustion from across the waters, approximately 1,116 miles away.

"He's fighting," Liz replied, which was what she seemed to always say. Nobody gave Whitney any concrete answers.

Whitney closed her eyes and swayed back and forth before catching herself against the mast. "I know he is. He's stubborn as ever."

"Yes, well." Liz very clearly wanted to get off the phone. "I'll tell him you called."

Whitney shoved her phone into her little backpack and stepped out onto the dock. Across the waters, music from the sailing party buzzed along. Currently, "No Woman, No Cry" hummed along while a pack of drunk sailors sang.

The party along the docks was made up of sailors who'd either raced in the Regatta or were involved in the sailing community. It was a fourth of a mile in length,

Sailing Home

dipping from one waterside bar to the next. Those with boats directly next to shore stood on them with beers lifted, laughing and chatting with those who passed along.

"There she is. Whitney Silverton!" A man onboard a sailboat extended his beer to toast her.

"Well, well. Look what the cat dragged in," Whitney said, smiling in spite of herself. "Jeffrey Masterson. I had no idea you were on this side of the Atlantic."

Jeffrey's smile showed off a big, gaping hole where his tooth should have been. This, Whitney knew, was a result of a sailing accident from thirty years ago. Whitney had been twelve or thirteen at the time.

She fell into Jeffrey's hug, remembering how he and her father had stayed up late nights, smoking, drinking, and playing cards. She had the sudden urge to ask if Jeffrey had quit smoking, but she held it back.

"Great race today, Bug," Jeffrey said, using a nickname nobody had used for Whitney in many years. "Your father would have been proud to see you."

Whitney laughed, blinking to keep the tears at bay. "I kept him informed on the whole thing."

"I'm sure he loves hearing from his Bug," Jeffrey said. "The two of you were inseparable. A dynamic duo if I ever saw one." Jeffrey turned back to call down into his berth. "Hey, Johnnie! Bug's here!"

Before long, Johnnie, another old friend of Tyson, jumped up from the berth and passed Whitney a beer. He and Jeffrey were soon deep into old stories about Tyson Silverton, most of which had occurred before Whitney had been born. Whitney had probably heard each of the stories ten to fifteen times, at least— but she allowed them to continue to tell them. Each word kept her father there with them on the coastline, at least in spirit.

After a bit of reminiscing and a beer, Whitney caught sight of a couple of guys she'd run around with in her early thirties. She bid goodbye to Johnnie and Jeffrey and leaped off the boat, humming with nostalgia and excitement. Maybe she didn't have to feel like a pariah all the time.

"Whitney Silverton!" This was Hank Poulter, a man who'd come up in the sailing world with Whitney. He hugged her and said, "It's been such a long time! How've you been?"

Whitney flipped her red hair behind her shoulders and grinned, genuinely glad to see Hank. He'd always been a scoundrel, but secretly, he had a heart of gold.

"I'm staying out of trouble," she told him. "Tell me that Violet's around here?"

Hank lifted his head slightly, searching the area around them. Sailors flocked in every direction. "Oh, you're in luck. She's right over here. Hey, Vi!"

Very soon, Hank's longtime girlfriend appeared and wrapped her arms around Whitney. She screamed, "Where the heck have you been all these years!"

Whitney laughed. "Gosh, it's been too long."

Violet gave her a slant-eyed look, one that told Whitney that Violet knew exactly what she was up to. "You've been hiding from us."

Whitney puffed out her cheeks. "I have not."

"Come on. Your relationship with Garrett has nothing to do with our relationship," Violet pointed out.

If only it was that simple, Whitney wanted to tell her. In truth, Whitney, Garrett, Violet, and Hank had palled around together for years. They'd been the perfect couple

Sailing Home

friends, often meeting them in ports and harbors across the Caribbean and the rest of the globe. For a long time, Violet had been the only female friend Whitney had in the community.

But after the breakup, everything in that world reminded Whitney of what she'd lost. Keeping to herself hadn't been a way to hurt those people. It had been a way to keep herself sane.

"Oh, but you're here, now," Violet said. "Come on. Let's get a margarita, like old times."

When they reached the line for margaritas, the bartender at the counter waved them up. "The winner drinks first and for free."

"And the winner's friend," Whitney quipped, nudging Violet.

The bartender nodded and began to make the drinks. Around them, the sailing party buzzed on beneath the brilliant pink sky. For a moment, Whitney could pretend that she and Garrett had met Violet and Hank at a classic sailing party— that she was younger and in love, with so much to live for. That her father was healthy.

"How have things been?" Violet asked as they perched near Hank's boat, where the rest of their crew sipped beers. "I mean, I've read about you quite a bit. All these races you've won? You're killing it."

Whitney tried to laugh. "I've been fine! Picking up jobs here and there. Racing the circuit."

Violet sipped her margarita, flashing her left hand forward. Sunlight caught both rings on her ring finger, and Whitney's heart dropped.

"I see you have some news?" Whitney asked, trying to sound exuberant.

Violet furrowed her brow before getting the hint.

"Oh! Right." She lifted her hand toward Whitney, showing it off. "We were basically married already but thought, what the heck? Why not seal the deal?"

Whitney's smile hurt her face. "Where did you do it?"

"Jamaica," she replied blissfully. "I would have invited you, but we kept it really small."

Whitney knew in her gut that they would have been best man and maid of honor if she and Garrett hadn't broken up. She would have loved it. She probably would have sobbed all the way through.

"I'm just so happy for you," Whitney said. "You and Hank were always the perfect couple."

Violet's face crumpled slightly, and she dropped her gaze to the ground. "I just hate what Garrett did to you."

Whitney waved a hand. "It was so long ago, now." She knew that was what she was supposed to say, even if she didn't feel it.

"I know." Violet sighed and sipped her margarita. "Gosh, I could drink these all day long! But I shouldn't. We're actually thinking about trying soon."

"Trying?" Whitney had no idea what she meant. It had been a long time since she'd had an extended conversation with a woman.

Violet smirked. "You know. Trying." She then hissed, "To get pregnant."

"Oh!" Whitney had basically forgotten that people actually did that. Her heart hammered with a strange mix of jealousy and fear. How could anyone raise a child? It seemed like the most difficult thing in the world.

"But not yet," Violet reminded her. "Today is all about the sun, the water, our boat, and plenty of margaritas." Her eyes glittered.

Sailing Home

Against all conceivable odds, Whitney found herself having a good time with both old friends and new. Violet introduced her to a few other sailors within their community, including another couple who, it seemed, had replaced Garrett and Whitney as their "favorite couple." The woman gushed about Violet and Hank's wedding.

"Hey! Rowan!" Hank called out to a passing sailor with wind-tossed black hair. He turned and gave Hank a blistering smile, calling back, "Hey there, stranger. Haven't seen you since Turks and Caicos."

Hank stepped up and gave the other sailor a bear hug. Violet leaned toward Whitney and whispered, "Isn't he handsome?" Whitney wanted to roll her eyes. Maybe this was another reason she'd stayed away. She didn't like the idea of being set up with someone.

Rowan joined their crew for a little bit, shaking everyone's hands until he reached Whitney. Instead, he bowed to her as though she were the Queen of England herself. "My, my. Whitney Silverton. It's good to finally meet you," he said. "I just read an interview with you in *Yachting Monthly*. I think the interviewer fell in love with you halfway through writing it."

Whitney really did roll her eyes this time. "Good to meet you. Were you in the race today?"

"I was. Probably about thirty boats behind you," Rowan told her, his grin widening.

He was handsome; Whitney wasn't immune to that. She sipped her margarita and forced her eyes away from the intensity of his gaze. He smelled like trouble.

"Oh. Hey, Cole!" Whitney stepped away from Rowan and the rest of the sailors, waving a hand toward her new twentysomething friend.

Cole blushed and lifted his beer in greeting. "Hi! Good to see you again."

"Likewise." Whitney glanced down the boardwalk for some sign of who he hung around with. "Are you by yourself?"

"My family went back to their apartment," he explained. "Thought I'd just wander around and try to keep out of trouble."

"Why don't you keep out of trouble over here?" Whitney said, gesturing toward her growing group.

Cole flashed her a confused smile.

"Come on," Whitney coaxed. Under her breath, she added, "You'd be doing me a favor. I haven't seen some of these people in years. Plus, the guy with the black hair is hitting on me big time, and he actually thinks he stands a chance."

Whitney returned to her place next to Violet and said, "Everyone, this is Cole. He came in what? Fourth place? Which is remarkable. He's clearly someone to watch in the sailing community."

Cole waved bashfully and sipped his beer. Violet and Hank gave him worthy congratulations before returning to their own conversation. Rowan didn't pay attention and continued to chat with another of Hank's friends, a guy Whitney had known back in the old days. Whitney was grateful to spend some time with Cole. He was just so gosh-darn sweet. Too sweet.

"Cole. Where are you from?"

"Martha's Vineyard," he replied, then took another swig of his beer.

"Ah. The Vineyard! I've raced in the Edgartown Regatta a time or two," Whitney returned. "Gorgeous scenery. But wow, you're pretty far from home, huh?"

Cole nodded somberly. "I've spent my whole life on the island. I figured it was time to see what else was out there."

"You were right about that," Whitney said.

"Yeah! You're on your way," Violet chimed in beside her. "The sailing community is a cozy one. We take care of each other."

Whitney wasn't entirely sure that was true, but she wanted to ease Cole's anxiety. Just as she prepared to ask Cole another question, however, she locked eyes with another man in the crowd.

Her heart shattered at first sight.

This man was Garrett Thomkins.

She hadn't seen him in over three years.

"Oh my God," Violet muttered under her breath. "I had no idea he was here."

"Yo! Garrett!" Hank called from their crowd. He walked out and gave Garrett the same bear hug he'd given Rowan. Throughout the hug, Garrett's eyes didn't leave Whitney's.

Whitney nearly forgot to breathe.

"Everyone, you know Garrett!" Hank said to the group.

Cole stepped aside to make space for Garrett. Again, he sipped his beer anxiously and blinked at Garrett with curiosity. True to form, Garrett ignored Cole altogether and continued to stare at Whitney.

"Hey, Whit."

Whitney could have screamed.

But instead, she said, "Hey." It was better to play it cool in these situations. Besides, hadn't she just stalked his social media that morning, curious about what he was up to? Now here he was, in the flesh.

"Good job today," Garrett continued. His muscles were threaded and looked bigger than they did in the photographs. He probably worked out at the gym a lot, one close enough to his new girlfriend's place.

"Thanks." She swallowed. "I take it you didn't race?"

"Nah," Garrett returned. "Just couldn't bring myself to miss the party."

"Right. My man never misses a party!" Hank cried.

Garrett was drunk. He swayed slightly as he stood with them, his bottle of beer lifted. Hank told Garrett a story about something that had happened out at sea a few weeks back, and Garrett guffawed. Whitney couldn't focus on the story.

Instead, she kept thinking:

How can I get out of this?

Finally, she returned her attention to Cole. "Oh, Cole. Do you need another beer?"

Cole shifted his weight nervously and inspected the bottom of his beer, although he obviously was low. "Sure, that would be great."

"Let's go get you one," Whitney offered. She stepped toward him, and together, they headed off for the nearest bar. Whitney's free hand quivered at her side. It was ridiculous, she told herself. She was a remarkable sailor; she'd stared death in the face and won. *Why was it that Garrett Thomkins filled her with such sorrow and fear?*

"Thanks a lot," Cole said as Whitney nabbed him a free beer.

"Don't mention it," Whitney replied. "I just wanted to get away from Garrett."

"Oh." Cole glanced back toward the group. The color drained from his cheeks. "Um. He's—"

Whitney followed his gaze to find that Garrett had

Sailing Home

decided to follow them. His hips were loose, shifting from left and right, and his smile was almost a leer. Whatever desire she'd had to speak with him one more time died right there on the boardwalk. He terrified her.

"Whit. Mind if we have a talk?"

Whitney stiffened. "I'm actually busy, Garrett. Maybe another time."

"Come on, Whit." Garrett stepped between Whitney and Cole and leaned to whisper in her ear. "I have so many things I want to tell you. So many things I want to apologize for."

Garrett's musk filled Whitney's nostrils, bringing nearly a decade of memories along with it. She shivered and stepped back, only for Garrett to follow along with her.

"Garrett. Step back," Whitney warned.

"I wouldn't be able to live with myself if I let you go without talking to you one more time," Garrett breathed.

"Garrett. Not here," Whitney growled. "Get away from me."

Suddenly, a hand wrapped around Garrett's large bicep and whipped him back. Garrett was too drunk to stabilize himself at first. He gaped down at Cole, who glared at him ferociously.

"Hey. Don't you speak English?" Cole blared. "The lady says she doesn't want to talk to you. What the hell is wrong with you?"

Garrett sniffed. His free hand formed a fist. Whitney wanted to close her eyes, suddenly terrified that Garrett would pound through Cole's skull. Instead, however, Garrett opened his lips and began to shake with laughter. Cole continued to glare at him, not pleased with being laughed at. Whitney was between so many emotions that her head spun.

Finally, Garrett turned back toward Whitney to say, "I like your new boyfriend, Whit. He's got spunk." After that, he turned back to saunter down the boardwalk. When Hank tried to hail him, he ignored him and continued to walk on by.

Overwhelmed with feeling, Whitney turned toward Cole and heard herself cry, "Cole? What were you thinking?"

Cole was pale as a ghost. He staggered back slightly.

"I had that, Cole. Do you understand me?" Whitney demanded. "The first rule of the sailing world is this: Stay out of other people's business."

Cole blinked at her, then said, "I'm really sorry." He sounded apologetic and out of place. He was far from home and completely out of his element.

But Whitney was too overcome with sorrow to say the right thing. She whipped around, nearly twisting her ankle as she went. Suddenly, she found herself sprinting back toward her boat, the only place in the world where she felt at peace.

Garrett was out there, and he wanted to talk to her. *What did he want to say? Did he want to tell her he'd messed up? That he wanted her back?* Her heart pounded with the depths of her loneliness, even as her soul told her a far different story.

Present-day Garrett was a drunk. He was cruel and manipulative. Maybe he'd been that way all along.

Chapter Five

"Cody? Or was it Chris? Could you take our picture?" A woman flailed her smartphone in front of Cole's face just as he was drawing the ropes tightly to adjust the sails. Annoyance flowed through him.

"Of course," he said, flashing her a smile. "I'll get to that right after I fix these sails. I want to get us to that cove over there. There will be plenty of photo opportunities once we get there. How does that sound?"

The woman considered this for a moment, clearly at a loss. Cole understood in a sense. This woman and her family paid an arm and a leg for a six-hour sailboat cruise around the British Virgin Islands. For the rate they paid, they expected the proverbial red carpet to be rolled out for them— everything from the perfect champagne and snacks to professional photography skills from the crew. This was laughable, given that Cole had hardly snapped more than ten photographs in his life. Still, he had to "give the people what they wanted."

They reached the cove, where Cole dropped the

anchor and beckoned for the smartphone. The woman and the rest of her very wealthy family gathered together, hugging one another in front of the jagged cliffside. Afterward, they tore off their clothes and leaped into the turquoise waters, crying out with joy. One of them said, "Carpe diem!" Cole couldn't help but smile. It was true that this was his life all the time, now. Other people's "paradise" was just his home.

Not that Martha's Vineyard hadn't been paradise, too.

"How are you doing?" Another of the crew members clapped his shoulder, watching the tourists as they snorkeled through the blue.

"Not bad," Cole replied with a shrug.

Under his breath, the other crew member said, "I know. The tourists are dead annoying. But the pay ain't bad."

It certainly wasn't. Cole was grateful to receive his cut when they reached shore later that evening, enough to tide him over the next week or two. As the tourists scrambled off to their next destination, he and the other crew members played music on a speaker and scrubbed the deck, wiped down the champagne flutes, and made fun of the tourists.

"Excuse me?" a crew member said in a high-pitched voice. "But are you quite sure this is the *Avenue Foch* champagne that we requested?"

Cole cackled and tossed his head back. "Was it?"

"Who knows? I bought something from the top shelf. That should be good enough for them."

"Nothing's good enough for them," another crew member said as he scrubbed a sponge over a bench near

Sailing Home

the stern. "They live in a state of perpetual anger and resentment. It's why they're all so skinny."

An orange sunset shimmered across the harbor. Cole headed into the berth for final inspection as the other crew members returned the cleaning supplies to the closet. Down in the berth, Cole caught sight of his reflection in the tiny, square mirror. He stopped short for a moment and blinked at the tanned and muscular man in the mirror. He was the spitting image of Aiden Steel.

Had Aiden ever wanted a life like this? The question often haunted Cole. Aiden had been a family man, forever head-over-heels with Elsa and the life they'd built. *But hadn't he craved the open seas? Hadn't he ached for whatever lurked on the far end of the horizon?*

Cole joined the others at the sailor's bar along the harbor. His beer sweated across the coaster as the other sailors in his crew talked about people he didn't yet know. Cole stretched his shoulders back, reminding himself of the wad of bills he'd just earned, which he'd tucked into his pocket. He would be all right.

"Hey! Cole?" A female voice rang out from the far end of the bar.

Cole and the rest of his crew turned and blinked at the beautiful forty-something redhead as she sauntered in. She looked like she owned the place.

"Hi, Whitney." Cole stood from his stool and furrowed his brow. "What's up?"

Cole's crew members' gazes were powerful, questioning why on earth Cole Steel knew Whitney Silverton. Whitney lifted a hand to greet them, then said, "Mind if we chat for a bit outside? I won't keep you long."

Whitney didn't give Cole a chance to answer before she turned around and headed back outside. One of

Cole's crew members whistled quietly. Cole turned and gave him a warning glare.

"I'll be right back."

Outside, Whitney leaned against the side of the bar and fiddled with a black choker around her neck. Cole leaned on the brick wall a few feet away from her, waiting.

Finally, Whitney spoke.

"I'm glad I found you," Whitney said. "I figured it was possible that you'd moved on to another island by now."

Cole lifted his shoulders. "I considered it but nabbed a job before then."

"Right. You have to go where the money takes you. I get that," Whitney told him.

Cole held the silence. He considered apologizing for the other night when he'd tried to get in the middle of Whitney and that drunk idiot at the sailing party. He didn't want to look pathetic.

Whitney wrapped a red curl around her ear. Timidly, she said, "I'm really sorry about my reaction the other night at the party."

Cole wasn't accustomed to apologies from anyone in the sailing community. He blinked twice, expecting a caveat.

Instead, Whitney continued. "I hadn't seen my ex in over three years, I'd been drinking, and I wasn't thinking clearly. But none of that serves as an excuse."

"Thank you for saying that," Cole managed.

Whitney shrugged. "It's been eating me up inside. It's rare to meet a guy as upstanding as you in the sailing community. I expect bad behavior, especially from guys like Garrett and Hank. And I certainly don't expect anyone to step up to help me. I never want

Sailing Home

Garrett to think I'm weak, especially now that we're over."

"I get it," Cole returned. "I've caught myself performing for my exes before. It always feels..."

"Like a waste of time," Whitney affirmed.

"Kind of. Because you spend so much of your life telling yourself they don't matter. And then suddenly, when they appear in front of you, it's like you have to be twice as good as you actually are," Cole said.

Whitney's eyes sparkled knowingly. "How old are you?"

"Twenty-eight," Cole offered.

"Ah! Then I guess you've had time for a heartbreak or two."

Cole chuckled. "Or two. Yeah. But they're all back on the Vineyard."

"So you escaped them. That's smart."

Was this really happening? A big-time sailor respected his sailing abilities, had sought him out to apologize for being rude to him, and now wanted to get to know him.

"By the way," Whitney began, her tone shifting. "I was just approached by an extremely rich guy to charter a sailing cruise through the Caribbean. Eight tourists, twenty-eight days. We start here in the Virgin Islands and head southeast, down through Guadalupe and Barbados, then head west toward the Dominican Republic."

Cole's eyes widened, impressed. "He wants the best of the best to take him there."

Whitney laughed. "I couldn't turn down the money. It's insane. The kind of thing that could set me up nice all winter long. The thing is, I need a crew." She locked eyes with Cole to add, "Would you be interested?"

"Seriously?" Cole was genuinely shocked. The other

crew members back in the bar would seethe with envy. What they made every day in their one-off cruises was probably pennies compared to this gig.

"Why not?" Whitney asked. "I told you that I like your style out on the water. You're respectful and kind, which is a rare thing in the sailing world and certainly appreciated when handling tourists. And— oh, you're probably one of the only people I'd be able to stand for twenty-eight days out at sea. What do you say?"

When Cole returned to the table, his crew members jabbed him with their elbows and asked if he had a "thing" with Whitney Silverton.

"What? No," Cole said, rolling his eyes.

But how could he explain the connection he felt? It wasn't romantic in the slightest. Instead, it was a kinship between two lonely individuals, neither of whom seemed to have any current concept of home. They were like extra puzzle pieces with no place to fit.

He couldn't wait to sail out with her. He couldn't wait to see the ocean through her eyes.

Chapter Six

"Ma'am? Excuse me. Ma'am?"

Whitney blinked from her reverie. She stood in just her socks in the middle of the security line at the Terrance B. Lettsome Airport, her shorts sagging at her hip. A TSA worker stood before her with a large knife lifted. His eyes were hard, confused.

"What?" Whitney stuttered slightly, realizing her mind had been somewhere in outer space. Besides, it wasn't like anyone had ever called her "ma'am" before.

"Ma'am. You can't take this knife on the plane," the TSA worker told her. He sounded exhausted, irritated, and very much like he wanted to go home.

"Oh. Right." Whitney eyed the backpack he'd removed the knife from. It hadn't even occurred to her that the knife she often took on sailing trips couldn't come with her to the skies above. "Can I leave it at the airport somewhere to pick up later? I'm coming back tomorrow or the next day."

"We have to confiscate it." Again, he looked at her like she was a delinquent.

"I haven't flown in over ten years," Whitney tried to tell him as he turned back to put the knife in a "safe place."

When he returned to the security line, he shoved her backpack over the counter and instructed her to put back on her shoes and her belt and "have a nice flight." Whitney glared at him, suddenly annoyed. Probably some time next week, she'd reach into her backpack to retrieve the knife and remember all over again that it had been "confiscated" and would never be used again. It felt so wasteful.

Whitney shrugged her backpack over her shoulders and wandered through the airport, through throngs of tourists. Many were scorched from their long days at the beach with their cheeks, and noses burned red from the sun. Some sipped lunch beers and stared at the Departures sign, their eyes glazed. Post-vacation blues.

Whitney grabbed an iced coffee and sat at her gate. Her knees bobbed around nervously as she waited. It was true what she'd told the TSA worker; she hadn't flown in over ten years. That trip had been with Garrett when they'd opted to fly to Athens and meet up with Garrett's other sailing buddy, a Greek guy named Stratos. The total travel day had taken nineteen hours. They'd been locked in a pill-shaped aluminum box in the sky, throttling through space and time zones.

When they'd reached Athens, Whitney had wept to Garrett that she couldn't imagine why anyone ever flew. "I'd rather sail home over the Atlantic." So that's what they'd done.

Aboard the flight, Whitney's anxiety mounted. The plane seemed old and clunky, and a part of Whitney didn't believe they would ever make it into the sky. When

Sailing Home

they reached cruising altitude, she beckoned a flight attendant to her seat toward the back of the plane and pleaded for a glass of wine. The flight attendant delivered it and asked for a whopping twelve dollars. Whitney's nose crinkled as she paid it. That was highway robbery.

"Do you live in Miami?" The older woman beside Whitney had a warm and inviting voice. The flower pattern on her shirt told Whitney she was a kind and loving woman, probably with several children she liked to bake for.

Whitney shook her head and sipped her wine. *Did she actually want to talk to anyone?*

"I don't. But my father does."

The woman brightened. "Ah! So you're going to see him."

"That's right."

"That's just lovely. I'm sure he can't wait to see his daughter," the woman continued. "Do you go home often?"

"When I can." Whitney cleared her throat and considered what she was about to put herself through. Soon, she'd be smack-dab in the middle of a strained conversation with Liz, probably choking down Liz's cooking. "But I've never flown back to Miami before. My father taught me to sail, so that's how I normally get up there."

"Oh! How long does that take?"

"About a week," Whitney replied.

"Goodness. You're really an adventuress, aren't you? I think I'd be too scared for something like that. I sometimes think that's why my husband left. He was so eager to run around the world and have adventures, and I was sometimes too scared to go to a party down the block."

Whitney's heart surged with sorrow and surprise. This woman had decided to offer up the depths of her sorrows, posing them almost like a joke.

"Hey. Socializing at a party down the block is a whole different beast," Whitney tried, stuttering slightly. "Sometimes out at sea, I go many days without talking to anyone. It's a relief!"

The woman chuckled and waved a hand. "Don't mind me. Most days, I think I'm happier without him. I think."

Whitney wanted to tell the woman just how much better it was that she hadn't stayed with a man who hadn't seen her for who she was. But instead, she sipped her wine and dropped her gaze to the ground.

Finally, Whitney mustered the strength to say, "My longtime boyfriend left me for the opposite reason, I think. He wanted to stay on land for a little while. He wanted an address and a refrigerator filled with leftovers."

"Oh, honey. The longer I'm alive, the more I'm sure that men don't know what they want."

"Maybe it's not a question of men or women. Maybe it's just people who don't know," Whitney pointed out.

"Just people," the woman considered, her eyes growing lost. "Maybe you're right."

* * *

Right before Tyson Silverton's big move to Miami, Tyson had assured Whitney, "I'll be out there on the water just as much as ever." That had been a big lie. No more than five years after his move, Tyson had sold his last sailboat and called himself landlocked. To Whitney, it was almost as though her father had given up their religion.

Sailing Home

Whitney sat in the back seat of a taxicab, whizzing through the sticky heat of Miami. Her backpack sat beside her, and the speaker system in the cab blared a rap song she'd heard a few times at the sailing bar in Road Town. The driver of the cab seemed uninterested in conversation, which was just fine with Whitney. She'd done enough "talking" with the woman on the plane, who'd never given Whitney her name, yet had revealed nearly all of her heart.

Tyson and Liz lived in a little one-bedroom house about ten blocks from Miami Harbor. Whitney stood before it, her hands looped around the straps of her backpack as the cab drove away with another chunk of her cash. A hummingbird, slightly earlier than his brothers who came from the north, hummed around the flowers in the front of the house. It was an idyllic scene; it seemed unrelated to Tyson Silverton's earlier life in every way.

Whitney pressed the doorbell and waited, holding her breath until a slight thump-thump came through the floorboards. Her lips curled up as she waited for her father; she wanted him to see just how happy he made her.

The person who appeared in the crack of the door, however, wasn't Tyson at all. It was Liz. Her eyes snapped around angrily as she rasped, "Why on earth did you ring the doorbell?"

Whitney balked. "Um. Because I'm here?"

Liz didn't open the door any wider. "Your father was up all night coughing again. He just fell asleep. You could have woken him up!"

Whitney's heart dropped into her stomach. "He just fell asleep. But he knew I was coming."

The second she said this, she was filled with regret.

His health was far more important than her spontaneous visit.

"I know. I know. I'm sorry," Whitney added hurriedly before Liz could screech at her. She closed her eyes and inhaled the milkshake-thick air. "Do you think he'll be awake sometime tonight?"

"Hard to say," Liz told her with a shrug.

"Well, I'm here till tomorrow afternoon," Whitney reminded her. "And I didn't sail, so I don't have anywhere else to stay."

Liz snapped her thumb back toward the inside of the house. "The couch is yours."

Whitney perched at the edge of the couch and faced the television, which now played through Liz's favorite four p.m. re-runs. Right now, *Everybody Loves Raymond* featured a grumpy Ray Romano and his wife, who seemed to put up with too much. Whitney had never been a big television watcher, but Liz seemed addicted to it. She sat with a bag of grapes and cackled at everything the characters said. Whitney wanted to remind Liz that she should quiet down and let her father sleep— but she wasn't keen to fight fire with fire.

Instead, she said, "I'm going out."

For hours, she wandered Miami, through the high-rises of downtown and westward toward Little Havana. There, she stopped for Cuban food at Versailles Restaurant, where she sat at a table for two and ordered enough food to feed at least three— yuca croquettes, ceviche, shrimp in creole sauce, vaca frita, and Cuban-style flan. The last time she'd visited her father in Miami, they'd eaten at this very restaurant until they'd stuffed themselves. They'd had to hail a cab to take them home.

It felt strange to do it alone.

Sailing Home

A family of four sat in the corner and feasted together. A little girl stood on the chair and announced that she had something to tell them. The mother urged the daughter to sit, but the father said, "Tell the world, honey! Tell them whatever's on your mind!"

"Are you going to need a box?" The server appeared at Whitney's table and eyed the still mostly full plates.

Whitney shook her head and said she needed more time. "Can I get a glass of wine, please?"

Whitney managed to stay out till nine, at which time she discovered a mostly dark house, save for the television that continued to play re-runs. Liz remained in front of it, dressed in her sleeping gown, her makeup stripped from her face. She eyed Whitney and said, "Can't imagine what there is to do out there for so long."

Liz returned to her room and left Whitney in the dark. The air conditioner toiled in the corner, buzzing against the pressing heat. Whitney donned a large sleep shirt and oversized shorts, then wrapped herself up in an afghan. Back on her sailboat, she often drifted to sleep in a split second, lulled by the subtle quake of the water. Here on Liz's couch, she felt stifled. Sleep wouldn't find her for many hours.

* * *

But the next morning, Whitney's trip was made worthwhile. She awoke to the chirping of pretty birds at the window, lulled in by Liz's flowers. In the kitchen, Liz prepared a pot of coffee and listened to a podcast about unsolved mysteries in Miami.

"That's scary," Whitney suggested as she poured herself a mug of coffee.

"Mmm." Liz seemed not to care what Whitney thought. "Your father's awake."

Whitney nearly leaped from her skin. "Can I bring him his coffee?"

"He's in his room with some tea and a bit of toast," Liz replied as she paused the podcast, clearly annoyed. "I'm sure he'd like you to say hello."

Whitney gripped her mug of coffee and hustled down the hallway, still in her oversized T-shirt and shorts. At her father's bedroom door, she rapped on the wooden door and waited for her father's joyous, "Come on in."

The man who sat upright in bed smiled at Whitney with the joyful smile of a much younger man. His cheeks held the slightest tinge of pink, and his two hands were wrapped around a mug of tea, solid and unshaken.

"Is that my Bug?" Tyson Silverton's deep baritone voice could have been taken from another decade. It was alive and vibrant, the stuff of long afternoons at sea.

"Dad!" Whitney clambered toward him, placed her mug on his nightstand, and carefully hugged him so as not to spill his tea. The man in her arms seemed stronger than she'd imagined; he was made of the kind of stuff that didn't fade easily.

It seemed impossible that this illness would take him. Obviously, the doctors had made some kind of mistake.

Tyson groaned and smiled, dropping his head back on his pillow. "You see what I have to do these days, Bug? They got me on tea only. No coffee."

Whitney wrinkled her nose. "What kind of injustice is that?"

"Exactly," Tyson spoke conspiratorially. "I oughta march right into that doctor's office and ask him if he thinks I'm a fool."

Sailing Home

"I'll come with you," Whitney said.

"Great. I need my Number Two out there with me." Tyson's smile fell the slightest bit. He sipped his tea and added, "My God, Whit. That win you pulled out at the Regatta was really something. I had Liz show me the video on the internet. That young guy out behind almost had you."

Whitney laughed. "I was a little nervous he'd catch me."

"Nah. You'd never let him," Tyson replied with a wave of his hand. "You were always too stubborn to lose."

"The kid is something special, though," Whitney continued. "He's twenty-eight and not as jaded as the others. Sometimes I think he might have a heart of gold. I invited him out with me in a few days. We're taking a bunch of rich tourists around the Caribbean for twenty-eight days."

"Boy, I don't miss those trips," Tyson said, his eyes misting with memory. "Those tourists always thought we were their slaves during those trips. Sometimes, they weren't so keen that I brought my little girl around with us. I always told them that that was nonnegotiable."

Whitney giggled. "I guess I wouldn't have known they didn't like that I was there."

"Nah. Besides, after just a few hours with them, you always charmed them," Tyson added. "And it was easier to get them to pay attention to orders with a little girl around. They wanted to be on better behavior."

"Unfortunately, I don't have any stowaway children onboard to keep the tourists at bay," Whitney joked.

"That's too bad," Tyson said, arching his eyebrow.

Whitney whacked the side of his arm playfully. "Are

51

you really going to give me the 'I want grandchildren' speech? You, Tyson Silverton?"

Tyson rolled her eyes. "Don't hate me, but I have to say this. I think you'd make a wonderful mother."

Whitney opened her lips to speak, only for Tyson to interrupt.

"With that said, I know what it's like out there on the water. It's hard to convince yourself to settle down. It took me years to decide to have a baby with your mother. I was—"

"Forty-four. I know," Whitney finished his sentence. "One year older than me."

"Of course, it didn't take your mother long to figure out that life wasn't for her," Tyson continued, digging his head deeper into the pillow. "Gosh, that was a lifetime ago. I can hardly remember what her face looked like. Probably a lot like yours, I suppose. However, there are hints of my own mother in your face, too. I prefer to see those." Tyson gave her a sheepish grin.

Their conversation continued deep into the morning. Whitney popped up frequently to grab more coffee, tea, and little snacks. Liz forced them to try the new vegan muffins she'd baked, which they pretended to like before wadding them up in napkins and shoving them in the trash. Here and there, Tyson coughed and wheezed— but mostly, he was his same-old, chipper self. He was eighty-seven years old, going on twenty-three. His jokes were just as snappy as ever.

When one o'clock rang out in the grandfather clock in the living room, Liz announced that it was time for Tyson's lunch and afternoon nap. Whitney wanted to scream at the woman and remind her that the man in bed beside her was just as healthy as ever. Maybe Liz and the

Sailing Home

doctor were in cahoots, telling Tyson how ill he was as a way to keep him on land. Maybe Whitney could sneak him out of the house and sail them both down south, where they could return to the old ways— just father, daughter, and the open sea before them. Adventures morning, noon, and night.

"I have to get to the airport, anyway," Whitney said.

"Oh, darn." Tyson sighed. "Our time went by so quickly."

"It really did." Whitney stood and bit hard on her lower lip. "I'm heading out with those tourists in a couple of days, and I have to prep the boat."

Tyson stuck out his finger and pointed it to emphasize his point. "You remember to put those tourists in their place if they get on your nerves."

"I'll do my best, Dad."

Whitney and Tyson hugged. All the while, Liz waited at the door, huffing with impatience.

"I love you, Bug," Tyson told her, clamping his eyes shut.

"I love you, too."

At the door, Whitney was overwhelmed with such goodwill that she stepped forward and wrapped Liz in a hug. Liz stiffened at Whitney's touch.

"He seems so good," Whitney said, her eyes widening. "Just as happy as ever."

Liz grimaced and crossed her arms over her chest.

"I'll come back after this next job," Whitney said. "Maybe we can even arrange a trip for him to come down to the Virgin Islands. I know the air would do him good."

Liz opened her lips to protest. But before she could, Whitney stepped out toward the sidewalk, her backpack thumping against her back. "Bye, Liz! Take care!" With just the flail of an arm two blocks over, she was off in a cab and headed for the airport. This time, she wouldn't fear the flight. This time, she would treasure every moment as they magically eased through the clouds, headed for the gorgeous islands beyond. Whitney felt so much happiness she almost had to pinch herself. She would never go that long without seeing her father again.

Chapter Seven

The sailing cruise planned to disembark from Road Harbor that Saturday, September 17th, at ten o'clock in the morning. Cole found himself on deck at five minutes past seven, finalizing the boat itself and listening to the morning squawks from overhead seagulls. Something was terribly peaceful about the harbor in the morning, the way the light played across the lapping waters and the boats tilted around like toys in a bathtub.

At the stern, Whitney wrapped her hair into a wild-looking ponytail. "You have a good week?" It took Cole a full two seconds to realize she'd addressed the question to him.

"Oh." Cole began to coil a rope around his loose palm, just as his father had taught him. *Was it professional to tell Whitney that he'd done little more than sail, drink at the sailing bar, and ask himself why in the heck he'd ever left Martha's Vineyard?* "Not that much. Just prepping for the trip."

Whitney flashed him a smile. "Come on. You must

have one or two stories for me. I remember being twentysomething in the sailing community."

Cole groaned. "Didn't I already tell you about my previous broken hearts? I'm not here to find yet another person to destroy me."

"Fair enough." Whitney's smile widened. "I can respect that."

With the sailboat finalized for the forthcoming trip, Whitney and Cole sat with mugs of coffee and waited for the tourists to arrive. Whitney glanced through the clipboard and asked, "Why don't we play a game? If you guess our tourists' very rich and famous-sounding last name, I'll buy you a beer the next time we're on land."

Cole grumbled. "Hmm. The name sounds rich and famous?"

"That's right."

"Are they actually rich and famous?"

"Not that I know of. But I'm not knowledgeable with celebrity gossip."

Cole dropped his head back and searched his mind for a famous last name. "Okay. What about Kennedy?"

"Nope." Whitney chuckled. "A Kennedy? Wow. You were shooting for the moon on that one."

"All right. Fine." Cole puffed out his cheeks. "You're going to have to give me a hint."

"All right. It starts with a B."

Cole grimaced. "B. B. Bach?"

Whitney rolled her eyes, already uninterested in the game. "Baldwin!"

"Ah. Right! Baldwin." Cole pretended to act enthused.

"It's so obvious," Whitney teased.

"Yeah. It was definitely my next guess," Cole said,

Sailing Home

rolling his eyes. "And what can you tell me about the Baldwin family to help me prepare?"

"Um. They're paying us a lot. So I guess that means they think we're like their hired help for twenty-eight days. I've found that it's better to make them think they're learning how to sail while actually doing all the work yourself."

"Good advice," Cole said.

"There are eight of them, which means they're going to get grumpy with each other and also with us," Whitney continued. "Oh, also. They're going to want to pretend that they're friends with us. But we have to remember—they're not our friends. They could turn on us at any time."

"Sounds ominous," Cole joked.

Whitney's eyes widened. "I've seen terrible things at sea."

"Is this where you tell me about the octopus that ate your friend alive?"

Whitney tittered. "All right, Cole Steel. Enough smart-aleck commentary from you. Snap, snap. Let's get ready for the Baldwins!"

* * *

All eight members of the Baldwin family stood before the sailboat. With the father, Kenny Baldwin, in the center and the rest of the Baldwins filtered out on either side, Cole thought they looked like the Brady Bunch or the Partridge Family. They were wholesome and American, most in polo shirts and many wearing all white.

"Welcome to *The Great Escape!*" Whitney proclaimed, citing the name of the boat she'd rented for the next twenty-eight days. "Please, step lightly over the walkway between the dock and the boat and follow my skipper here to your bedrooms below deck. Remember, everything on a ship like this has to be on the smaller side — so don't be surprised if you don't find a California King mattress down there."

The Baldwins tittered at her joke as they stepped, one after another, across the walkway. The first was Kenny Baldwin, a man who looked to be in his mid-fifties with salt-and-pepper hair and muscular legs, probably from hours on the tennis court. He snapped his hand forward and shook Cole's, saying, "Nice to meet you, Sport."

Cole mumbled, "Nice to meet you, too," before he turned on his toe and led Kenny, his wife Bethany, and two of their three adult children down into the stern.

"It's up to you to decide who sleeps where," he told Kenny Baldwin, parroting the very words Whitney had told him to say.

Kenny stroked his recently shaven chin and eyed the multiple beds, many of which were tucked into closet-sized rooms beneath the top deck. "Twenty-eight days like this, Bethany," he said to his wife. "Do you think we can manage it?"

Bethany's laughter was nervous. If Cole had to guess, she seemed like the type of woman who always had to tell Kenny that he was right, even when he wasn't. Probably, she'd manipulated herself into always believing he was right. It was easier that way.

"Yo! Dad!" A guy around Cole's age hollered from the other end of the berth and said, "This'll be perfect for my little family." He gestured toward a bunk bed and a double bed tucked up beneath a slanted window.

Sailing Home

Kenny puffed out his chest. "Yes, Gregory. You, Buffy, and Roger take that room."

"Roger!" Gregory called up to the deck, where a five-year-old stood giggling next to another Baldwin. "Come down here to see your bed!"

Cole leaned against the wall, watching as Gregory showed the bunk bed to his son, who was dressed in a crisp polo. Cole couldn't help but feel for the kid, forced to spend twenty-eight days with only adults.

"Where will Marshall and I go?" An adult daughter in her early thirties pouted at her father.

"Natalie, you and Marshall should take that bunk bed over there," Kenny said, pointing.

"A bunk bed?" Natalie half shrieked.

"We're out at sea, darling," Kenny told his daughter. "You and Marshall can make do for a month, can't you?"

Natalie grumbled to herself as she clacked in high heels toward the bunk bed.

Kenny's eyes then scanned back toward the light that shone in from the top deck and hollered, "Aria? Where in the heck are you?" Under his breath, he added, "I wouldn't be surprised if she jumped ship."

"Dad. You promised to behave around Aria," Natalie muttered.

Kenny twisted his face into a smile as another daughter rushed down the ladder. She seemed to be the youngest of them all, no more than twenty-four or twenty-five, and her blond hair spilled in all directions as though she hadn't bothered to brush in many weeks. Her dress hadn't been ironed, and her lipstick was smeared.

As Aria lifted her eyes to smile at her siblings, Cole's heart shattered at her subtle beauty. There was a ruggedness to her, something completely alien in a family like that.

"All right, Sergeant," she said to her father. "Where shall I sleep for the night?"

Kenny grumbled and pointed toward a single bed tucked away in the corner. "That's for you, Aria. Naturally, when we first planned this trip, we all thought we'd have another member of our group with us."

Aria's eyes rolled back into her head. "Isn't it better he's not here? This place is already cramped, and he was the type of guy to always bring at least three suitcases, plus another bag for his nightly skincare regime."

"Gosh, I wish I could get Marshall to do a skincare regiment," Natalie moaned.

Kenny glowered as Aria dropped her single suitcase on her single bed. Cole tried to put two and two together. Obviously, Aria had just broken up with someone who was "Baldwin-approved." Aria seemed so un-Baldwin. Cole imagined the couple had gone together like oil and water.

But it was just a guess.

"Come on, everyone!" Whitney called from up on deck. "Let's get our safety meeting started. After that, Cole and I will sail us out of the harbor and into the open seas. I hope you're ready for the sail of your life!"

One after another, the Baldwins clambered up into the sunlight. Cole hung back, ensuring their safety. Aria came last, locked eyes with Cole, then wrapped her hands around the rungs of the ladder.

"Hi. I'm Aria. What's your name?" She was the first to ask.

"Oh. I'm Cole." Cole wiped the sweat from his palms. "Nice to meet you."

Sailing Home

"And you." Aria puffed out her cheeks and glanced up. The sunlight glowed across her cheeks, making her look angelic. "I hope my family doesn't give you too much grief. They can be..."

"Aria?" Kenny called from above. "Are you dillydallying? Didn't you hear what our captain said? She's a female captain, you know. I thought you'd like that."

"Well, I guess you can already tell how they can be," Aria said under her breath right before she climbed into the sunlight.

Cole's heart pounded with intrigue. He inhaled, exhaled, and shook his head to clear the cobwebs. It couldn't happen. It was stupid to even dream about it.

Up on deck, Whitney had begun the brief yet very important safety meeting. She outlined the top rules of the boat, showed them where the boat safety kit was located, showed them where the life jackets were, how to work the small cooking stove, where the food and beverages were located, and how to maneuver around the boat safely.

"There are ten of us on this boat," Whitney reminded them. "We have to watch out for each other, especially when we're out there." She pointed out toward where the harbor was swallowed by the ocean.

Whitney gestured for Cole to demonstrate a safety procedure. As she passed him a life vest, Cole lifted his eyes to find Aria's peering out at him curiously. She stood next to her mother with her hands on her hips, both terribly bored and beautiful at once.

"Cole?" Whitney hissed, forcing him to jump back into their rehearsed safety instructions.

"Right." Cole snapped the life vest over his chest and turned to face Whitney. Together, he and Whitney were like puppets, performing for the Baldwins. When they finished the safety instructional course, the Baldwins' eyes were glazed over with boredom.

"Let's get this show on the road," Kenny ordered, clapping his hands.

"Everyone, take a seat!" Whitney called as she and Cole hustled around, untying ropes and opening sails. Cole was caught up in the easy sportsmanship of the launch and soon lost himself in it. Soon after, cool wind washed over his face. Kenny lifted both arms toward the sky and hollered, "YEAH!"

The other Baldwins followed suit, echoing what their father already thought.

And at that moment, Whitney skidded past Cole and whispered in his ear, "Be careful. Remember what I said about these people? They're not our friends. Not even the beautiful ones."

"Aye aye, Captain," Cole said, saluting her.

It wasn't like he would ever do anything like that. He would never do anything to taint his reputation, especially since he was so new in the sailing world.

"Gorgeous start!" Kenny howled, his arms outstretched as they breezed toward the opening of the harbor and toward the enormity of the ocean beyond. "What a perfect morning for a sail!"

Chapter Eight

It was their seventh day at sea and too early yet for the Baldwin clan to have emerged from their bunks. This left Whitney and Cole alone in the silence of the morning, tightening the sails, brewing coffee, and gazing out across the hazy blue. After so many days together, working as the crew versus the Baldwins, Whitney had begun to think of Cole as her kid brother— a guy she could tease and chat with. He made her feel totally at ease. This played in contrast to the Baldwin children, who seemed to use every opportunity to argue.

"So far, so good?" Cole asked, interrupting the quiet as he stepped past Whitney to pour himself another mug of coffee.

"Surprisingly, yes." Whitney shook out her red hair and added, "They bicker and fight with each other to no end, but they haven't done anything outrageous yet."

"We still have three weeks," Cole reminded her. "Plenty of time for everything to go south."

"I love your optimism. It reminds me of me," Whitney teased.

That day, the plan went like this. They would tie up in Guadeloupe, buy provisions, and hit the beach. Guadeloupe was a gorgeous place, one that the Baldwins had apparently never seen. As the champagne, wine, dairy, meat, and seafood were running low, Cole and Whitney saw this as a perfect opportunity to prepare for the week ahead.

"And while we're shopping, we can have some quality time away from the Baldwins," Whitney reminded him as she continued to write the list of groceries.

Cole laughed, his eyes shining. Whitney searched for something in that face of his, a clue that he was falling for the youngest of the Baldwin siblings. But there was nothing. And as far as she'd seen, he'd kept his distance. Maybe it was all in her head, a hunch that made her wary.

They docked the boat at ten in the morning. The Baldwins dressed in their bathing suits, grabbed their towels, and padded off the boat, already squabbling about what they wanted to eat for lunch. Whitney had told them to hit up the beaches in Pointe des Châteaux, where Whitney and Cole planned to meet them after their grocery trip. They would find something delicious there. In fact, Whitney's father had known several of the Pointe des Châteaux restaurant chefs back in the old days, many of whom had passed on their know-how to mentees.

"You ready, skipper?" Whitney asked Cole.

Cole laughed and scrubbed his hand through his salt-tinged hair. "Let's get this cart on the dock."

The cart was loaded with empty champagne and wine bottles, empty bottles of sparkling water, divided recyclables, and a large bag of trash. The bottles made the

Sailing Home

cart extra heavy, and Whitney winced as they heaved it—proof that she wasn't as strong as she'd once been.

Whitney and Cole strutted down the dock, wheeling the cart behind them and waving at other sailors. Two big-bellied men in their sixties or seventies waved hello and called, "Bug!" Whitney vaguely remembered them from one long-ago trip or another she'd taken with her father. She waved back, her red hair flipping out behind her.

"Who are they?" Cole asked.

"Friends of my father," she explained. "It's funny. Feels like no matter which harbor I'm in across the world, I always run into someone who knows him."

"That's insane. I thought it was crazy that every sailor knew my father on Martha's Vineyard. This is next level."

Whitney laughed, her heart lifting. Her legs felt loose and athletic beneath her. It would be a beautiful day.

* * *

After recycling the goods, purchasing more, and reloading the boat with their new provisions, Whitney and Cole changed into their swimsuits and hailed a taxi to take them to Pointe des Châteaux.

"Are you two on vacation?" the cab driver asked, eyeing Whitney and Cole in the rear-view mirror.

"Oh. It's our honeymoon, actually," Whitney said spontaneously, clasping Cole's hand.

The cab driver's eyes widened with shock. "Oh. Um. Well. Wow. A honeymoon!"

Whitney shivered with laughter as Cole tried to suppress his own beside her.

"You know what?" Whitney said, pushing it further.

"Everyone said, 'Jameson? You can't marry a guy twenty-five years younger than you just because his name is Jim Beam.' But you know what I told those people?"

"Um. What did you tell them?" The cab driver seemed very unhappy that he'd ever asked.

"I told them, 'Watch me!' And ever since, Jim and I here have been happy as clams. Right, Jim?"

Cole's eyes were damp with laughter. "That's right, Jameson. We're happy as clams."

"You know what?" the cab driver began. "Love is love! No matter what!"

"That's right!" Whitney cried, raising her hand with Cole's.

When they reached the beaches outside Pointe des Châteaux, Whitney paid the cab driver and tipped over thirty percent. The cab driver thanked her profusely and said, "Have a beautiful honeymoon, you lovebirds." He then drove off happily, whistling so loud that you could hear it over the motor.

Cole shook his head at Whitney, shorting with laughter. "That was really something, Jameson."

"Come on, Jim Beam. Let's go find our Kennedys."

The Baldwin family had sequestered off a gorgeous area of the beach, mere feet from one of the natural hot water baths of the area. The mother, Bethany, sat sunning with her older daughter, Natalie, while the son, Gregory, played Frisbee with Marshall. Where was Buffy? Ah, there she was— walking out from the nearby beach bar with two margaritas in her hands.

Kenny sat in the hot water pool by himself while Roger scampered around, often interrupting the Frisbee game.

Only Aria was missing.

Sailing Home

"Where's..." Whitney began.

"There." Cole stretched his finger toward the ocean, where a tiny head could be seen far out, directly beside a rock that surged two stories into the sky.

Whitney gave Cole a side-eye. She wanted to say how extraordinary it was that he'd spotted Aria so far out to sea. But she held her tongue.

"Hey, Cole?" Whitney adjusted her sunglasses on her nose. "I'm going to head down the beach and give my dad a quick call."

Cole nodded knowingly. She'd told him about his cancer diagnosis and about how vibrant he'd seemed when she'd spent some time with him. "Tell that epic man I said hello."

"He'll be like 'who?'" she quipped.

"Ha. Ha." Cole rolled his eyes and headed toward the Baldwins. It was the first time Whitney noticed that he'd placed a book under his arm, eager to catch some time alone. Whitney hardly met anyone in the sailing community who enjoyed reading, so this warmed her soul.

Whitney called her father on video chat and waited as the call rang out across the waters. A little while later, Liz's face appeared. She had her lips pointed toward the ground. Whitney had probably made her miss some of her show.

"Whitney?" Liz's voice was sinister.

"Liz?"

"Your father is asleep."

"Oh." Whitney wanted to shrug it off, but truthfully, she felt crushed. She hadn't managed to video chat with her father in four days at that point. She wanted to see that big, eager smile again. She wanted to remind herself how good he looked.

"And don't ask me. I'm not going to wake him up!" Liz said.

"I wasn't going to ask you," Whitney shot back.

Here she was, at odds with her stepmother while on one of the most beautiful beaches in the world. It figured.

"I'll try to call him later," Whitney said doubtfully. "But tell him I love him, won't you?"

Liz grumbled to herself. "Of course. We'll be seeing you." She then hung up the phone.

"We'll be seeing you," Whitney muttered to herself. "What a weird woman."

Whitney slipped off her shoes and held them at her side as she wandered through the sand toward the Baldwins and Cole. Her head pounded, threatening a good, old-fashioned headache. She needed a big glass of water and a moment of quiet. She needed her dad.

Closer to the Baldwins, she noticed movement. A woman thrashed across the beach, laughing. Whitney paused, watching as the woman lifted her phone and tried to take a photograph.

It took a second for Whitney to realize that the subject of the photos was supposed to be Cole, who evaded them each time.

Cole extended his hands, panting with exhaustion. "Please. No photos," he begged Aria.

"Come on! I'm trying to remember my life," Aria said, pouting.

Behind them, Kenny Baldwin stood up from the natural pool and placed his hands on his hips. For a guy in his fifties, he sure had a good six-pack.

"Hey, Cole?" Whitney called out, ending the strange chase.

Cole yanked his head around. His eyes were electric

Sailing Home

and full of fear. He dropped down, collected his book, and headed back toward her. He looked like a little kid who'd been caught doing something he shouldn't have.

"What's up, Captain?"

Whitney rubbed the ends of her hair. "I have to head back to the boat."

"Oh. We just got here."

Whitney shrugged. Her stomach clenched and unclenched. "I'm just not in the mood anymore."

"Oh." Cole palmed the back of his neck. "Did something happen with your dad?"

"No. Nothing like that," Whitney lied. "But I'll start prepping dinner. Good to get a head start."

"You want me to come back with you?"

"No. Just enjoy yourself," Whitney told him. "It's our honeymoon, after all. One of us should have some fun."

Cole snorted and rolled his eyes. Whitney's sorrow lightened. At least they could pretend everything was okay within the short confines of their jokes.

Back onboard *The Great Escape*, Whitney stripped down to her swimsuit and lay across a bench, gazing up at the sky above. Fluffy clouds ambled past, and the blue of the sky seemed almost impenetrable— with a density she couldn't understand. She'd spent so many hours of her life staring at that sky.

That night onboard the ship, they planned to have tapas: fresh bread from a Guadeloupe bakery that she and Cole had found, olive oil, olives, multiple types of cheeses and sausages, hummus, and dried tomatoes. It would take a lifetime to arrange the items beautifully, especially for a family of eight. Luckily, Whitney had that kind of time.

Whitney turned on her favorite playlist, mostly songs she and her father had listened to during their travels through the eighties. Each song felt almost like an assault on her heart. Still, the songs brought back memories of him. She could almost pretend he was just below the deck.

A little before five, Whitney hustled downstairs to find her phone charger. There, she hunted through her bag, tossing T-shirts and shorts across her comforter. Just as she found it, she heard familiar voices up on deck. They were harsh with anger.

Whitney remained very still, listening. Slowly, the voices grew loud enough for her to understand them.

"You know what kind of person you're supposed to be with. Someone who fits in our family, Aria. Someone like Benjamin."

Aria howled. "I told you! I never loved Benjamin! I was only dating him to appease you, which is frankly disgusting. You should be glad I dumped him. Everyone should be glad I dumped him! You know, he sent me one hundred red roses last week. Isn't that disgusting?"

"Aria." Kenny Baldwin sounded terribly frustrated. "You're my only child who isn't married. It keeps your mother and me up at night."

"That isn't exactly my problem, is it?" Aria shot back.

"That's my girl," Whitney muttered to herself.

"I'm just saying," Kenny said. "You should not fraternize with that sailor. I see the way you look at him."

"Oh my God! Are you seriously telling me not to talk to the guy who's aboard this super tiny ship with us?" Aria cried.

"You aren't just talking to him, Aria. You know what you're doing."

"Dad. Seriously?"

Kenny seemed flabbergasted. "I just want you to

watch yourself, Aria. You're a Baldwin. You have to remember that."

"Dad. You barely got me to go on this trip with you guys," Aria reminded him. "Just lay off me, okay? I'm still just about this close to abandoning the family forever. You have to remember that."

Chapter Nine

Whitney had charted their course on an old-fashioned nautical map, which she'd tacked to the interior of the office that she and Cole shared. Within that office, they kept equipment they didn't want the Baldwins to tinker with, snacks they didn't want to share with the Baldwins, and other important essentials, like their wallets and cell phones.

Cole nibbled at an oatmeal cookie and traced their course on the map with his finger. Already, they'd been out to sea for twelve days, which meant they had only sixteen to go. As Whitney said, they were "in the thick of it."

Cole swallowed the last of his oatmeal cookie and brushed the crumbs from his lap. The clock on the little desk read 14:17. This meant 2:17 in the afternoon. Whitney insisted on using military time in all things sailing-related. It was easier that way.

Out on deck, the Baldwins stretched out beneath the splendor of the sun. They enjoyed their post-lunch haze,

Sailing Home

many with books propped on their laps or magazines reflecting the afternoon light. Roger played quietly in the corner, moving cars across the deck. That morning, Kenny Baldwin had told Roger to "hush up and behave," and Roger had taken this to heart. He wasn't the kind to mess around with their grandfather's will.

Cole couldn't remember a single time he'd been frightened of his grandfather Neal. He was grateful for that.

Aria perched on the far end of the deck, hanging her feet loosely over the side of the boat. She seemed to be sketching something on a little notepad. She cocked her head in concentration and tied her hair up to avoid distraction. A small voice in the back of Cole's mind wondered what she might be drawing. Another voice told him that he couldn't worry himself with stuff like that. He'd seen the way Kenny Baldwin had looked at him in Guadeloupe. He'd nipped their silly flirtation in the bud.

Still, it was rare to see a woman sketching on a paper pad. It was rare to see anyone do much more than look at their phone. Cole appreciated that.

"Cole!" Whitney appeared in the doorway of the little office. Her red hair tore violently through the air. "Come see!"

Cole followed Whitney out on deck, where she raised a pair of binoculars to her eyes and muttered, "Yep. Just like I thought." She passed the binoculars over.

In the distance, several sharp and glittering fins darted across the waves. Cole's heart surged. Suddenly, one of them whipped into the sky— showing its slender torso and pointed nose.

"Dolphins," Cole breathed.

"Should we get closer?" Whitney asked mischievously.

Cole leaped to adjust the sails and direct them leftward toward the school of dolphins. Meanwhile, Whitney addressed the Baldwins and said, "We have a bit of a surprise for you." She said it as if she and Cole had planned it; Cole knew this was necessary to make the Baldwins think that they'd pulled out all the stops for their rich clients.

One by one, the Baldwins stood and followed Whitney's pointed finger. Bethany, the matriarch, said it first. "Oh my gosh! Dolphins!" The others followed suit, gasping as they drew closer and closer.

Aria leaped toward the edge, her curly hair bouncing out of its updo. "Oh, we should swim with them!" She then turned and locked eyes with Cole at the helm as though she'd sensed his gaze.

Cole dropped his eyes immediately.

"That's not a good idea. Too many things can go wrong in the open ocean like this. One is that they can bite you. Let's just watch and enjoy the moment," Whitney affirmed.

"My gosh. I never thought of that!" Bethany cried.

As they approached the school of dolphins, the marine mammals grew curious and splashed their fins, swimming closer. They lifted their strange yet friendly faces from beneath the surface and spoke to the people on board. To Cole, the noise sounded like a monster in an alien movie. The Baldwins, however, thought the sound was "sweet."

"It's like they're talking to us," Natalie said, crouching down so that her face was only a few feet from the speaking dolphins.

Sailing Home

"They're trying to," Whitney said. "Although humans haven't discovered the secret to their language quite yet."

They watched the dolphins play in the deep blue, lifting their noses, making clicking and whistling sounds to say hello as everyone watched in awe. Once they had disappeared about fifteen minutes later, Cole stabilized the boat in a sheltered bay nearby. Many of the Baldwins jumped in for a quick swim to cool off in the sweltering heat.

Whitney stepped back toward the helm and muttered to Cole, "Why don't you take a break? Go for a swim?"

"Are you sure?" Cole asked. Whitney gestured out and said, "Yeah, we'll just sit here for a bit and enjoy the gorgeous views."

"What about you?"

Whitney shrugged. "I grew up doing stuff like this. Besides, you've worked hard this morning. Go and enjoy the water?"

Cole jumped at the chance. In a flash, he stripped his T-shirt from his shoulders, donned his swimming shorts, and dove into the turquoise waters from the top of the boat. The dive was almost perfect, shimmying him through the depths until he lost all the oxygen in his lungs. He then kicked his way to the surface and broke up a good twenty feet from the sailboat. From that distance, he could see Whitney peering in the opposite direction, watching the Baldwins. Cole was alone.

So far from home, shifting gently against the ocean's waves, Cole felt his heartbeat slow. He closed his eyes and floated on his back, pointing his feet toward the blue sky. For a long time, he focused on just his breathing. Inhale, exhale. Inhale, exhale.

Since he and Whitney had taken the Baldwins out to

sea twelve days ago, Cole had felt surprisingly okay. He hadn't awoken in the middle of the night, sweating through his shirt and quivering with fear. He hadn't ached for his father, heavy with regret. He'd simply existed to sail. It had been enough.

Cole swam freestyle around the boat and treaded water about ten feet away from the Baldwins. It was like watching a bunch of kids. Even Kenny looked vibrant, his face twisting into a smile that seemed almost unnatural on his face.

Perhaps the Baldwins weren't the nicest bunch in the world. But right then, Cole could pretend that they were just people. They'd fallen in love with the natural world, just as he had.

Suddenly, a figure burst up from the waves directly in front of Cole. Water splashed across Cole's face and smothered him. Aria's laughter exploded over him, joyous and unencumbered.

Cole sputtered, coughing out the water as Aria lifted herself onto her back and floated. "I got you!" she teased.

Cole grumbled inwardly. "What did you think of the dolphins?"

Aria's hair wafted beautifully in the water directly beneath her head. "They're gorgeous, of course. But they know it, don't they? They're like the cheerleading squad of the ocean. I think they're up to something."

Cole laughed even though he'd told himself not to make himself so open to Aria. Under his breath, he said, "You might have something there."

"Right? They're just too beautiful, you know?" Aria giggled and twisted herself through the waves.

Cole swam around her and headed back for the boat.

Sailing Home

Aria chased after him, grabbing his foot playfully and tugging at him. Cole detested this kind of play in the water; he'd heard of too many drownings. He gave her a look, which made Aria chortle.

"Uh-oh. Someone's angry," she teased.

Suddenly, Kenny Baldwin turned his head to catch them. His eyes glittered with malice.

"Whitney?" Cole called, his voice wavering. "You about ready to get going?"

Whitney leaned over the side of the boat, eyeing him curiously. She hadn't seen the Aria incident.

"I think we can give it another ten minutes or so," Whitney told him.

Aria had noticed her father's anger and begun to swim back to her sister, who'd grown bored of swimming. Roger, dressed in a life preserver, bounced around playfully.

Cole pulled himself back up the ladder and grabbed a towel to wrap around his shoulders. Whitney muttered, "Did something happen?"

But Cole didn't want to drudge up any bad blood. "Nah. Not really."

Whitney's smile widened. "You have to learn to stop and smell the flowers every once in a while."

"I'll make a note of that. Thanks," Cole offered sarcastically. "Gosh, you've really taught me a lot on this journey, you know?"

Whitney rolled her eyes. "You keep this up, and I'll make you scrub the deck just for the fun of it."

"Aye aye, Captain."

Out in the water near her sister and her mother, Aria's gorgeous eyes continued to watch Cole's every move.

Embarrassed, Cole hid in the office and stress-ate an oatmeal cookie. Crumbs stuck to his wet legs and feet.

Stay professional, Cole, he told himself. *Don't make yourself look like a fool. Your career depends on it.*

Chapter Ten

Something about the ocean so late at night was thunderous. It stretched out as far as the eye could see, black as ink and pulsing gently with the breeze. Whitney stood with her hand around the mast and gazed at the smattering of stars, billions of billions in just the Milky Way alone. *"The best place to see them is out here, Bug,"* her father had said. *"We get a view the rest of the world can't ever know."*

"Whitney! You want a glass?" Natalie destroyed Whitney's reverie. She wavered in the center of her family, her white dress fluttering as she lifted a glass of wine toward the stars.

"How can I resist?" Whitney shot back, turning to rejoin the party, which had been raging since sunset. The Baldwins were fine drinkers; anyone in the sailing community would have been impressed with what they could put away without batting an eye.

"Whoa!" Natalie grabbed a glass and poured the wine while Buffy messed with the Bluetooth speaker, boosting the volume.

"That's it," Buffy said, clearly pleased with herself as "The Rhythm of the Night" pumped through the air. "That's the one."

"She always plays this one when she gets drunk," Natalie said under her breath to Whitney. "It's her only tell."

"Rhythm of the night. All right! Yeah, yeah." Buffy bounced her head along to the beat.

"Where are we right now?" Natalie asked Whitney as Whitney poured the rest of the wine bottle into Natalie's glass.

"We're just north of Grenada, if you can believe it," Whitney returned. She was vaguely proud of how well she'd charted the course, allowing them ample time at the various islands, sidled with plenty of time at sea. Kenny Baldwin was bound to give her and Cole a killer tip.

"Grenada..." Natalie echoed, trying to roll it the way someone who spoke Spanish correctly would. It sounded terrible. "Gosh, we've been to so many places."

"Rhythm of the night!" Buffy continued to sing with her eyes closed.

For whatever reason, Whitney felt overwhelmed with goodwill. She lifted her drink and grinned at the Baldwins and Cole, all of whom sat across the deck and against the stern, chatting and moving their arms around like excited puppets. Cole locked eyes with her and dropped his chin in recognition. Beside him, Marshall continued to explain the intricacies of Bitcoin. If Whitney had to guess, Cole was the least likely person in the world to care about Bitcoin. *Good luck to him*, she thought.

"Who else wants a bratwurst?" Kenny asked, standing to retrieve the chilled meats from the cooler.

Cole stood to grab the little barbecue cooker, which

Sailing Home

they'd used for a number of meals since they'd boarded *The Great Escape* twelve days ago.

"Marshall, I know you want one," Kenny began, counting out the brats. "Gregory? Buffy? Peter?" He then paused, watching as Cole lit the flame and adjusted it so that the full barbecue cooker heated evenly. "You need help, Cole?"

Cole blinked up at Kenny. "I'm good, Mr. Baldwin. Thanks a lot."

Kenny brought his shoulders back. "Great. Good." He glanced down at the cooler and added, "Would you like a brat?"

"That would be fantastic, Mr. Baldwin. Thanks."

Whitney's heart opened wider at Cole's remarkable politeness. She couldn't imagine him ever offending anyone.

As the last bars of "The Rhythm of the Night" petered out, Aria burst from the stern, her hair like lightning in the dark. "It's my turn to pick a song!"

Natalie groaned. "None of your hipster stuff."

"Yeah, Aria. Remember that the whole family has to like it," Bethany said.

"Everyone in the family really likes that night rhythm song?" Aria demanded.

"You know what it's called," Natalie snapped.

"Girls!" Bethany chided, crossing her ankles. "You sound just like you did when you were teenagers. Won't you ever grow up?"

"Here it is. This is the one." Aria ignored her mother and switched on her song. She then stretched out her arms wide to the starry sky above and began to sing.

"You're just too good to be true. Can't take my eyes off

you. You'd feel like heaven to touch. I want to hold you so much."

Midway through her solo, Natalie and Buffy burst in with their own renditions. The two Baldwin sisters' and sister-in-law's voices joined and floated across the night sky. For a moment, Whitney marveled at the beauty. Then her eyes dropped to Cole, who stared at the ground like it was filled with snakes, prepared to bite him.

The lyrics. It seemed so obvious, now, that Aria played this song only to mess with Cole. Whitney scrunched her nose and watched as Aria twirled in circles, latching her hand to Natalie's and Buffy's and looping them around. She flowed magically. It was likely she'd once been a dancer or a gymnast. She had full control.

Petrified, Whitney turned to check on Kenny Baldwin. To her relief, he was deep in conversation about real estate with his son, Gregory. His right foot tapped along to the music, but he seemed unaware that Aria was trying to put on a little show for Cole.

"You know? I kind of hate this song," Whitney said loudly enough for Buffy to hear.

"Why's that?" Buffy called back over the screaming speaker.

Whitney shrugged. "It reminds me of my ex."

It did. Garrett would have detested that song with every fiber of his being.

"Oh! Oh my God!" Buffy grabbed the speaker and turned off the sound immediately.

Aria and Natalie hissed.

"What are you doing?" Natalie cried.

Buffy wagged her eyebrows knowingly. Whitney suddenly felt "in on" their girl club.

Sailing Home

"It reminds her of her ex," Buffy hissed.

Natalie's lips formed a round O. Her eyes damp, she whispered, "Oh, you poor thing. How long has it been?"

Whitney shrugged. *Was it pathetic to say three years?* She figured it probably was.

"Just over six months," Whitney lied.

"No!" Buffy cried. "How long were you together?"

"Ten years," Whitney returned. This was the truth, and it made the Baldwin sisters sadder than ever.

"Oh my gosh. And you never got married?" Natalie whispered.

Whitney shook her head. "We talked about it." *Had they?* Yes. But for Garrett, each conversation had been a massive joke. Whitney hadn't exactly been in on the joke, but she'd laughed anyway.

How stupid she'd been.

"Men are sometimes very difficult to pin down," Buffy muttered knowingly. Her eyes flashed toward Marshall, Natalie's husband, who continued to converse with Cole about Bitcoin. "I mean, it took Nat, what? Five years till you got engaged?"

Natalie blushed before turning toward Aria. "Aria was basically engaged to Benjamin."

Aria crossed her arms, clearly annoyed. "I was the one who broke things off with Ben. Not the other way around."

"Did he cheat on you?" Buffy asked her little sister, feigning worry.

Aria rolled her eyes. "I cheated on him."

Both Natalie and Buffy gasped with horror. On the other side of them, Bethany leaped from her bench and cried, "What am I hearing? Aria Baldwin, will you repeat what you just said?"

Whitney grabbed her glass of wine, refilled it to the top, and moved toward the berth. Cole mouthed, "Thank you," just before she disappeared. Downstairs, all she could hear was the muffled hissings of Bethany, Buffy, Natalie, and Aria as they argued about Aria's apparent infidelity.

Whitney's bed was latched away in a private bunk with a door. With the glass of wine on the shelf and her entire body on the bed, she yanked the door closed and exhaled all the air from her lungs. It was difficult for her to forget that, for a split second, she'd felt like one of the Baldwin sisters. Beyond that, she'd actually liked it.

What if she'd had a sister? Probably, that sister would have picked her back up after Garrett had cheated on her. She'd have forced her to eat real food and go out dancing and flirt with other men. She wouldn't have allowed Whitney to stew in her own sorrows for more than three years.

Whitney's cell phone buzzed in her back pocket. Surprised that she had service at all, she grabbed it and glanced at the message, almost without thinking about it first.

> LIZ: Whitney, I wanted to let you know that your father passed away this morning at 9:30. His pain is over.

Whitney gaped at the words. They seemed so sterile and far away from any concept of reality she understood. Her thumbs remained poised over her screen for a long time.

A horrible screeching sound came from between her ears. It felt like someone had smashed her head with a sledgehammer. She dropped her phone and rubbed her temples, watching her screen until it faded to black.

The words continued to ring through her head.

Passed away. This morning.

At 9:30.

His pain is over.

What was going on?

It wasn't clear how long Whitney blacked out. Once she came to, she grabbed the phone to reread the message. It was only then that she realized that Liz hadn't texted her until three thirty. This meant that her father had died, and it had taken Liz six hours to remember, *"Oh. He has a daughter. Maybe she'd like to know."*

Whitney seethed. Her eyes closed, she shifted to-and-fro as the boat rocked beneath her.

Her father, the brightest shining star she'd ever known, had passed on.

Her father, the great Tyson Silverton.

Her father was the only friend she'd had throughout her childhood.

How was it possible that he'd died?

Her heart cracked at the edges. She dropped back on her mattress, wondering why she hadn't started crying. Her eyes hadn't caught up to her emotions yet. Maybe the trauma of this had destroyed the connection between her body and mind. *Was that physically possible?* She thought abstractly about looking it up online.

She could search:

Have you ever been so sad that you couldn't cry?

Or:

Am I broken because I can't cry?

Or:

Am I a monster?

Whitney placed the flat of her hand against the door beside the bed and continued to rock with the boat. *Where was she, exactly?* She'd lost track. Last she remembered, she and Garrett had been somewhere in the French Riviera. For dinner, they'd feasted on a baguette and several types of cheeses and shared a bottle of wine. God, they were happy.

But that had been years ago, hadn't it? Long before her father's diagnosis.

She was becoming one of those people who couldn't keep track of time.

She slowly drew the door between her small bedroom and the rest of the berth. Upstairs, people bantered and sang along to a speaker. Whitney shook her head as images crashed over her. The Baldwins; Cole Steel; the wide-open ocean; her forty-third birthday, spent alone.

And then, her stomach filled with stones.

Her father was dead. She willed herself to remain in that thought for a moment. Everything she'd known about the world had now shifted. Nothing would ever be the same again.

Chapter Eleven

Up on deck, a bottle shattered. Whitney was jolted back to reality, her ears craning for an explanation.

"Everyone! Watch out! Don't step on the glass!" Bethany slurred her cry.

Whitney heaved toward the ladder and yanked herself toward the smattering of skies above. Midway through the portal, the sound of Kenny Baldwin's anger exploded across the black seas.

"You! Get away from her!"

Cole stuttered, "I didn't do any—"

"Don't you dare talk back to me! Do you know how much I spent on this trip? It's more money than you'll ever see in your life," Kenny spat.

Whitney's heart sank. She leaped to the deck to find herself at a distance from where Cole stood, his hands lifted to protect himself. The Baldwins gathered in a semi-circle around him as Kenny Baldwin stood just a foot in front of him, a single finger pointed. Kenny's eyes flashed with anger, lit up from the cooking stove on deck.

Whitney was petrified. She searched through the sea of onlookers and finally discovered Aria, toiling between her sister and her mother as her father ripped into Cole. It was clear that none of the Baldwins knew what to do.

Finally, Cole splayed his hands in front of him, clearly exasperated. "Listen, man. I was just over here listening to Marshall blabber on and on about Bitcoin."

"Hey—" Marshall began.

Cole slashed his arm through the air. "Your daughter just came up to me! Sat next to me! What was I supposed to do? Move? Not sure if you noticed, Mr. Baldwin, but this boat isn't that big."

"I swear, if you keep this up..." Kenny slurred angrily.

"What? What are you going to do? Because I'm tired of you looking at me like you're going to kill me, just because—" Cole blared.

"Cole!" Whitney called from behind the Baldwins.

But just then, Kenny flailed forward, prepared to trounce Cole. He kicked his feet wildly behind him as he punched forward. All at once, one of his feet met the cooking stove and cast the hot coals backward across the deck. Several of the Baldwins leaped back, shrieking.

"Oh my God!" Natalie cried.

Cole and Whitney normally kept the rolled-up sails secured and tidy on the upper area of the deck, out of the way. Unfortunately, in the drunken haze of that night, the Baldwins had decided to move the sails to the ground so that they could sit on the raised platform.

The coals scattered across the sails.

It was like tossing a match on a pile of paper.

The hot coals flashed fire across the sails. They licked up the sails, forming a fire that seemed much too big for such a small sailboat. Whitney, who was already struck with grief, watched the fire as though it was something separate from her. It couldn't possibly be happening.

The Baldwins' screams flung out across the dark ocean. Abstractly, Whitney imagined the newspaper headlines that would inevitably follow this:

The Baldwin Billionaires' Sunken Vessel - And The Woman Whose Fault It Was

Any newspaper article would list Whitney as the captain of this ship. It would also list her as alone in the world, her father dead and her ex-boyfriend long gone. "No children. No meaning."

In the midst of Whitney's wild yet reflective haze, Cole leaped into action. He threw himself across the sailboat, grabbed a large bucket, filled it with water, and flung the water over the burning sails. The fire turned to steam in an instant, leaving behind sails with charred endings and brown patches. They looked like marshmallows in a bonfire.

For a long moment, as the steam filled the sailboat and filtered out across the water, the Baldwins were speechless. Whitney urged herself to head toward Cole and bark some orders, anything to get this boat back on track.

Suddenly, Aria burst from her sister and rushed toward Cole. "Cole!"

But Cole placed the flat of his hand between himself and Aria. He shook his head angrily and then lifted his eyes toward Kenny Baldwin. Everyone was silent with disbelief.

The silence stretched on for fifteen seconds, maybe more. Whitney shivered with fear. She felt completely disconnected from her body. Beneath her, the rocking of the boat seemed unnatural. She'd never craved solid ground more.

Suddenly, Buffy cried, "Oh my God! Look!" She lifted a finger to point out to sea. As the steam from the fire cleared, a massive rock jutted out from the sea directly in front of them. Around that rock, several smaller ones raised their backs toward the sky.

Whitney gaped at the rocks, petrified. Her head spun as the Baldwins continued to scream and cry.

Whitney had to get them out of this. Cole had already done enough.

She leaped toward the helm and began to direct them as best as she could away from the massive rock. If they didn't change course immediately, the bow would shatter against the rock and toss them into the frothing waves. They would be done for.

As Whitney steered them away from the rock, her mind slowly returned to her full force. With this, however, came multiple questions— none of which were comfortable to answer. *How long had she been in the berth, hiding away? How much time had she allowed to pass?* Now, she clearly remembered telling Cole that she would monitor the course for the night so that he could rest and celebrate.

It was her fault that they'd lost the course. It was her fault they were up against this mighty array of rocks.

"Everyone, sit down!" Whitney cried.

Terrified, the Baldwins did as they were told. The intensity of the moment made them quiet.

Whitney managed to manipulate the sails well enough to clear the massive rock, plus several others that appeared just behind and to the side. It was almost like

Sailing Home

playing a video game and narrowly avoiding that which was bound to kill you. Unfortunately, this current "game" was life or death.

This many rocks in a row meant one thing: they were much closer to shore than she'd anticipated. Whitney racked her brain for some understanding of how she'd let this happen. *Hadn't she been a worldwide sailing champion? Hadn't she felt this otherworldly connection to the sea, the wind, and the sky?*

Whitney yanked the boat rightward, heaving them away from another flatter rock. Whitney gasped for breath as sweat pooled across her back. The Baldwins' eyes were large and white, like saucers. She held their lives in the palm of her hand.

In the distance came the glinting lights of a nearby port. It was hard for Whitney to imagine which island they were closest to. Quickly, she turned her head to call out to Cole, "Hey! I need you on the map. Which port is that?"

But just as she finished, Cole whipped an arm out to point at yet another rock. This one had snuck out of nowhere, hidden on the other side of another rock that Whitney had narrowly missed. The bow of the vessel skidded across the rock almost in slow motion. The noise was horrendous, guttural. The boat sounded like an animal or a monster crying out in pain.

"Oh my God! We're going to sink!" Natalie shrieked. She roped her arms around her mother and wept against her shoulder.

For a moment, Whitney thought Natalie was right.

They skidded off the rock and tilted slightly to the right before dropping back down into the water. They were now cleared of most of the larger rocks but still had a smattering of a few in front of them. Whitney clung to the helm with all her strength. Her fingers ached with tension.

"Everyone! Remain seated!" Cole cried, his hands up so that the flats of his palms faced the Baldwins. He stood with his legs wide and opened a compartment on the damaged side of the boat so he could peer along the body of the hull. Even from across the boat, Whitney could see all the color drain from Cole's cheeks. He turned his head so that his eyes locked with Whitney's.

It was only a matter of time before this boat sank.

"We have to get to the harbor!" Whitney called. Her voice sounded guttural, so unlike her own.

"Everyone. Put on life jackets!" Cole whipped open the compartment near the little office and began to pass out bright orange jackets.

Buffy Baldwin bent down to snap the life jacket around little Roger. Roger was giddy and laughing as though the ride was like a roller coaster, rolling over waves and rocks.

"I think we should pray!" Bethany Baldwin chirped. She seemed mere seconds from bursting into tears.

"Shut up, Bethany," Kenny glowered. "The only person who should be praying is that woman over there at the helm. If we survive this, she's going to pay. Big time."

Whitney couldn't bring herself to care. She focused herself on the lights that burned brighter and deeper as they got closer. The density of the harbor was incredible, stretching out across countless decks. Whitney remembered the feeling of returning to the harbor with her father as a young girl. As she'd strutted around the boat, adjusting the sails and helping out, her heart had cried out

Sailing Home

for whatever this new reality would prove itself to be. Every new port offered new adventures. She'd always believed that until she hadn't anymore.

"Should we go get our things?" Natalie wailed to her husband, Marshall. "My Tiffany jewelry is just on the nightstand."

"Oh my God! My Lange und Söhne Watch!" Buffy cried. "I have to go..." Buffy rushed toward the berth, followed by Natalie and Bethany.

"I need you all to remain on deck!" Cole cried.

But it was too late. They'd transitioned to the mass pandemonium phase, wherein the selfish Baldwins played out the full extent of their materialistic desires.

"Honey! Can you please hunt down my Patek Philippe watch?" Marshall called from above berth, eyeing Whitney. "Remember it was three million, darling. Nothing I'd like to sink into the sea."

Whitney's heart rattled in its rib cage. She could hear the slushing water as it slowly drifted through the boat's hull. No matter how she shifted the sails, they continued to slow.

"Cole?" Whitney called, hunting for him. She'd lost him as he'd walked downstairs to retrieve the Baldwin women and force them back on deck. They appeared, carrying their expensive belongings and tugging suitcases into the dark air.

"I'm here," Cole said, his voice jagged.

"We might need to send out a distress signal," Whitney said, no longer caring that the Baldwins could hear everything she said.

Cole turned to gaze out across the glass of the harbor water. "We'll make it," he said, his voice brazen with confidence. "Four or five minutes longer. Just keep us going."

"We're losing speed!" Whitney reminded him.

"Nothing we can't work with," Cole said. He walked around and stood to the right of her, allowing him a better view of how the boat tilted away from its injury. Under his breath and into her ear, he added, "The water's coming in, but it isn't coming so quickly that we can't manage it. You kept us away from the worst of the rocks. Remember— you saved us."

Whitney's heart shattered. Cole, being Cole, continued to compliment her, even in her darkest moments. The fact that they'd faced the rocks at all had been Whitney's fault. She would never forget that. Cole knew it, too.

Over the next five minutes, the Baldwins kept quiet. All eyes were pointed toward that sparkling harbor. All ears were filled with the horrible sound of the water as it rushed over the jagged pieces of the side of the boat. Whitney's legs quivered beneath her, but she willed herself to remain standing. This was it. It was now or never.

Whitney located space on the dock and quickly eased the boat toward it. Cole leaped from the deck and hurriedly tied the boat to the dock, his motions quick and articulate. The silence felt like an overwhelming bubble that was about to pop.

Suddenly, Natalie rushed toward the side of the boat and vomited into the water. Gregory let out a single sob as he gathered Roger in his arms and stomped off the boat and onto the dock. Aria and Bethany hustled downstairs to retrieve the rest of their belongings, which they passed

Sailing Home

up to the deck. Each time Whitney spotted Aria, the girl's eyes were glassy with horror.

Whitney shouldered the majority of the night's guilt, but it was clear that Aria took on some of that guilt, as well. She'd pushed the Cole situation too far. *Why? Had she wanted to "prove" herself to her father? Had she wanted to show off?*

With their belongings successfully off board, the Baldwin family surged away from the boat, dragging their suitcases so they bounced along the wooden slats. Not one of them said goodbye. Even Aria was far up in line, rushing as quickly as she could away from *The Great Escape*.

Away from Cole. Away from the mess of this once-in-a-lifetime sail across the Caribbean.

Away from the horrors of what Whitney had done.

Whitney staggered toward the side of the boat and opened the compartment to peer down at where the water that had gotten into the boat sloshed. The deep and black water was a perfect symbol for all she'd done. She thought for a moment that she would throw up, just as Natalie had.

But suddenly, a voice tore through her ears.

"Listen to me."

Whitney lifted her eyes to find Kenny Baldwin's. He stood on the dock above her with his finger pointed in her face. His skin was blotchy with fear and rage.

"What you did here tonight is unacceptable. You put my entire family in danger. And you will pay dearly for what you've done."

Whitney's lips parted. *How could she tell him just how brokenhearted she was? How could she tell him that she'd never wanted this? That it was inconceivable to her that she'd messed up so badly?*

"I—"

"I swear to God, if you give me any kind of excuse, I'll..." Kenny began dangerously.

Cole leaped onto the dock and glowered at Kenny. "I think it's about time you get out of here."

Kenny turned his attention to Cole. "I don't think it's up to you what I do or not, son."

But Cole stood his ground, puffing his chest out until he seemed about three times as muscular as Kenny Baldwin. Despite all his "nice guy" charms, Cole was clearly powerful and athletic. There wasn't a lot he couldn't do.

After a terrible moment of silence, Kenny muttered something to himself, turned on his heel, and stomped down the dock. Whitney watched as his white polo shirt disappeared into the haze of bright lights across the harbor and the rest of the island town.

Whitney shivered and wrapped her hands around her elbows. She felt like a lost and forgotten child. The first sob finally came out of her, overly loud and heavy with sorrow. After that, more sobs came, fast and loose. She shook uncontrollably as she continued to sob. They sounded unlike anything she'd ever produced before.

Cole remained on the dock and extended his hand out for Whitney to take. "Come on, Whit. Come on. We'll get through this. You got us to safety! Look!" He jumped on the dock, proof it was land or at least connected to it.

But Whitney couldn't calm down. Her legs shook so violently that her knees clacked together. She closed her eyes against another crash of sorrow and dropped her head back so that all the blood rushed toward her feet.

Sailing Home

She'd nearly killed an entire family.
She was ruined.

Everything in her life she'd once cared about was gone.

All at once, Whitney's body flailed to the floor. Gray and black spots filled her vision until all she could see was darkness.

Chapter Twelve

The most renowned and powerful female in the sailing world lay unconscious across a broken sailboat. Her arms flung out beyond her head, and both legs were askew. Cole Steel stood on the dock above her, incredulous. He hadn't caught his breath in what felt like hours.

Cole knelt at Whitney's head and called her name. "Whitney!" But she was knocked out cold. He pressed two fingers to her throat and felt a faint pulse. Her lips were parted as though she was about to say something.

The other boats around where they'd docked for the night were empty. Cole wasn't sure how late it was. Ten? Eleven? Closer to midnight? His best bet was to run back to shore, hail a taxi, and get Whitney to the hospital. But dammit, where was his phone? He leafed through his pockets and found nothing but his wallet and a receipt from a laundromat.

"Bear with me," Cole whispered as he knelt lower, positioning one arm beneath Whitney's knees and another to support her head, neck, and shoulders along his left bicep. Despite her toned build, she wasn't terribly heavy. Cole lifted with his knees and then stepped delicately onto the dock, grateful, yet again, for dry land.

As Cole headed back toward the boardwalk, Whitney remained unconscious. Cole racked his brain to understand what had gone wrong. One minute, he'd been tipsy on champagne and listening to the blabbering of Marshall about all things cryptocurrency. Cole even remembered telling Marshall that, yeah, he would have to hook him up in the cryptocurrency world. Gosh, maybe Cole had been drunker than he thought.

Around him, the Baldwins had seemed in good spirits. Aria had been dancing a lot, drawing her other sister and sister-in-law into the center to twirl one another around. It had seemed like good old-fashioned family fun.

Until suddenly, Aria had twirled herself directly to Cole's corner, made eyes at him, and dropped herself directly beside him. With Marshall continuing his monologue about Bitcoin, Cole hadn't been able to budge. Aria's shoulder had dug into his bicep; her fingers had fluttered along his.

After that, the world had exploded.

But where had Whitney been? Why had they gotten so far off course? It didn't make any sense. Had there been a mistake with the equipment?

Cole burst onto the boardwalk and staggered forward, his breath catching. Several tourists and other sailors stood at the neighboring sailing-themed bar, sipping pints of beer and bobbing their heads to "Margaritaville." The song sounded like a nightmare.

"Please! Help!" Cole called as he stomped toward them, trying to keep Whitney comfortable.

At first, nobody at the bar noticed him at all. Or maybe they noticed him and just discredited him as yet another drunken sailor, one they could ignore.

"Please!" Cole appeared at the edge of the bar, which was thick with people. He wanted to force his way through and ask the bartender for help, but it would have taken ages. "Please, will someone call the ambulance?"

Finally, a man in his forties turned away from a conversation with a beautiful woman about Cole's age. He looked disgruntled and sunburnt from a long day at sea.

"What's the matter, son?" he asked Cole, stepping away from his table to hear. He didn't sound pleased to do it.

"She's unconscious," Cole said. "We had an accident."

The man turned back and called out, "Can someone bring a bench with a cushion on it?" His voice broke through the crowd with authority. "Hey! Someone. Now. A bench."

A few seconds later, two other men in their forties carried a bench with a light green cushion across it. They positioned it directly in front of Cole and helped him splay Whitney across it gently. Meanwhile, the first man busied himself with calling 434, which was the emergency number for ambulances in the area.

"Which island is this?" Cole asked suddenly, lifting his head up to stare into the eyes of one of the men who'd brought the bench.

"You're on Grenada, mate," the man replied in an English accent. "What did you think?"

"Are you about to be knocked out from alcohol like

Sailing Home

your friend here? Are you that confused?" the other chided.

Cole felt volatile with anger. He closed his eyes for a long time, bent down, and stroked the hair across Whitney's sweat-stained forehead.

"Hey. Wait just a minute." The guy with the English accent sounded conspiratorial. "Isn't that Miss Whitney Silverton?"

Cole's stomach clenched with fear.

"I think you're right about that," the other guy blared. "Hey! Look here!" He waved to the guy just finishing the 434 phone call and pointed at Whitney's unconscious face.

"Stop pointing in her face," Cole blared.

The guy hung up the phone and gazed down at Whitney for the first time. "I'll be damned. It is her. Isn't it?" He shot the question to Cole.

"It doesn't matter who she is," Cole said ominously. "She needs help. I told you. We had an accident. The boat in the harbor needs to be removed from the water as soon as possible, too."

"You're telling me that the great Whitney Silverton had an accident?" the man with the phone said. He shook his head in disbelief, then turned his muscular body around to call out through the crowd. "Hey! Hey, Garrett! I have a present here for ya. A big surprise."

Cole's jaw dropped. For a few frantic seconds, he tried to come up with a plan to carry Whitney away from these horrible people and their gaping smiles. But soon after, Garrett wormed his way through the crowd and appeared at the edge of the bar.

"What are you going on about?" Garrett asked the friend with the phone. Midway through his sentence, however, his eyes dropped toward the woman stretched out on the bench and widened with surprise.

"Oh my God. Whitney?" He hustled to her side, his cheeks turning white.

What were the odds that Whitney's ex would be on the very island they basically had to "crash land" on? Of all the Caribbean Islands, he'd chosen that one. Had Whitney been awake, she probably would have said something like, *"There's my good luck again. Sailors always said never to bring a woman onboard a ship. This is payment for my recklessness."*

Suddenly, the ambulance screamed toward them, flashing its lights across the sunburnt faces outside the bar. Cole lifted a hand toward the ambulance as it parked, and the EMT workers burst out to grab a gurney.

"Wait a minute," Garrett said, eyeing Cole. "I know you."

The EMT workers spoke hurried Spanish as they set up the gurney beside the bench. Cole's Spanish remained limited, although it was on his list of "things to work on."

The man who'd originally offered to call the EMT had the best Spanish of all of them. Cole had him explain that Whitney had collapsed after an "accident out at sea."

"I think she's in shock or something," Cole said. The man nodded and explained this to the workers.

The EMT shuttled Whitney toward the waiting ambulance. Cole leaped after them, grateful to be away from the "boys club" at the sailing bar. But a split second later, Garrett called out, "Hey! I'm coming with you."

Cole stopped short and turned, his anger boiling over. *First Kenny Baldwin, now this?* He'd had just about enough of men who felt they were owed something.

Sailing Home

Besides, Whitney had told him all the gritty details about how Garrett had cheated on her after ten years together. It was despicable.

"You're not going with us," Cole retorted, his voice menacing.

"Like hell I'm not." Garrett laughed aloud as he remembered. "It's just like back on BVI. You were all ready to stand up for Whitney. What? Are you in love with her or something? I think she's a little old for you, but I'm not one to judge."

Cole made fists and glared at this horrible man. "Whitney doesn't want anything to do with you, you understand me?"

"Who are you, anyway?" Garrett demanded. "Are you here to speak for Whitney? Because I'm here to tell you—" And here, he stuck out his finger and jabbed it into Cole's chest. "That Whitney and I had a whole life together. We lived through thick and thin. I think that makes me much more qualified to get into that ambulance with her. Don't you think?"

Garrett stomped around Cole, headed for the ambulance. Cole rushed back and forced himself in Garrett's way, screaming, "Get away from her!"

Garrett's fist was the size of a small boulder. Cole was semi-conscious of that boulder as it swung up from Garrett's side and hit him hard on his left eye and upper cheek. Cole's scream erupted over the Grenada Harbor and across the ocean. Even his knees couldn't take it, sending him to the ground.

"Hey! Wait a minute!" Garrett called out to the EMT workers.

But the EMT workers waved their hands and spoke in Spanish. From where Cole remained on the ground, he deduced that the EMT workers weren't ready to let some guy who'd just started a fight onto a moving ambulance. With the back doors closed, they stepped into the front of the ambulance, restarted the siren, and tore off through the night.

Garrett staggered back, screaming expletives at the moving ambulance. Cole couldn't have imagined something more absurd than screaming at some Spanish-speaking EMT workers in a language they didn't understand long after they'd fled the scene. But then again, Garrett seemed like the type to do that.

Garrett turned around with murder in his eyes. Cole forced himself back to standing, scared that Garrett would come over and start kicking him. Instead of attacking Cole, however, Garrett headed back toward the bar, ruffling his salty hair.

Cole wasn't in the clear yet. In the wake of Garrett's attack, his head rang like a bell. He raced toward the nearest street and flailed his arm for a taxi. All he could do was drop into the back of that taxi and say, "Hospital! Hospital! Emergency!" The taxi driver nodded, his eyes turning to slits.

They were on their way.

Chapter Thirteen

Whitney hadn't woken up on land since her stint on her father's couch a few weeks back. That morning in Miami, with her cheek shoved hard against the stained pillow, she'd ached to be back out on her boat, rocking gently as the sun crept overhead. That had been the final day she'd seen her father alive.

The morning she woke up at the hospital in St. George's General Hospital on the island of Grenada, the air felt terribly still. The starched sheets around her felt as stiff as paper. The curtains had been drawn so a grayish light filled the room.

Land. She was back on land. But it took her quite a while to figure out why and how.

Her eyes adjusted to the gray light, widening as she inspected everything from the rickety chairs to the horrible beige curtains to the clock on the wall, which told her it was nearly eleven in the morning. Whitney couldn't remember the last time she'd slept so late. The vibrancy of the harbor and its sailors ordinarily didn't allow that sort of sleep.

Her body felt very strange, as though her mind remained at a great distance from the rest of herself. She lifted her fingers to check the connection; everything seemed to be working, if slowly.

A sigh, followed by a snore, erupted through the quiet space. Whitney turned her head a smidge to find Cole Steel collapsed in one of the rickety chairs. Slobber glinted on his chin.

"Cole?" Whitney cried out in surprise. She hadn't yet put the pieces of the story together and felt flabbergasted to see him. "Cole, what is going on?"

Cole snorted awake, grunted, and leaped to his feet. "Whitney!" He sounded genuinely surprised.

What had happened? Could she just come right out and ask it? Or did she have to play it cool and ease them both into it?

But suddenly, Whitney became very aware of something that made the situation ten times more confusing.

"Cole, what happened to your eye?"

Cole winced and dropped his chin toward his chest. "Oh. Um."

"It's a huge black eye!" Whitney continued, her heart fluttering. In the sailing community, a black eye wasn't exactly an uncommon thing. Men liked to throw their arrogance around in a way that often started fights. Still, Cole wasn't one of those kinds of guys.

"Yeah. Um. I imagine it is by now," Cole said with a shrug.

"When did it happen?" Whitney demanded, searching her memories.

Sailing Home

Images flashed through her mind. Kenny Baldwin, standing in front of Cole on the deck of *The Great Escape* with a finger pointed in his face. Then hot coals flashing across the sails. A rock shimmering out of the darkness. Panic. Screaming. Whitney shivered as she cowered in bed.

"Did Kenny Baldwin do that to you?" she gasped.

Cole wrinkled his nose. "No. It's a long story."

Whitney gestured across the hospital bed. "I have time."

"But how are you feeling? I want to know that first."

Whitney dropped her head against her pillow. She still felt terribly heavy with exhaustion.

"When you fainted like that, I was terrified," Cole told her softly.

Whitney didn't remember fainting. The last she remembered was Cole tying the ropes to the dock as the Baldwins scampered to dry land.

"The boat. Is the boat all right?"

"I took care of it," Cole explained. "As soon as I got to the hospital last night, I used a pay phone to call the harbor and explain what happened. They removed the boat from the docks and have it stored. The guy I talked to gave me a phone number for a repair shop. I have an appointment with them tomorrow at around noon."

"Tomorrow." Whitney sounded wistful as though tomorrow might never come. "Thank you for taking care of that."

"It's nothing," Cole told her.

"It's everything."

They held the silence for a long time. Cole's bruise was purple, black, and green. Whoever had struck him had had a really cruel right hook. She opened her lips to ask the question again, but Cole spoke before she could. He knew he couldn't get away without answering it.

"I ran up to the bar to ask for help. The man who called the ambulance recognized you, and then Garrett appeared."

Whitney was too tired to fully comprehend this story. It was hard to imagine that her body had been splayed out in front of these men, unconscious and open to interpretation.

"I don't know why he was here," Cole continued, his eyes widening. "He came after you, trying to get in the ambulance. I stood in his way."

"And then he punched your lights out," Whitney finished.

The corners of Cole's lips quivered into the smallest of smiles. "Your ex is really something."

"You can say that again." Whitney's heart ballooned at the story. Cole had stood up for her yet again.

"I just can't believe he was there at all," Cole said, pounding his leg. "And then, to make matters worse, he came to the hospital after the fight. When I saw him in the waiting room, I told the woman behind the counter that he had punched me. She ordered security to take him away immediately."

"Oh my God." Whitney dropped her face in her hands. The man she'd loved for ten years had been dragged away from the hospital, probably calling them a whole lot of horrible names along the way. What a nightmare.

"What are you thinking?" Cole asked softly.

What could Whitney say? She finally snorted. "It figures."

Sailing Home

"Why do you say that?"

"I was having the worst luck of my life yesterday." She shook her head so that the greasy strands of her hair washed over her cheeks. "Anything that could have gone wrong did go wrong."

They held the silence for a little while. Both of them were clearly ashamed of what had happened onboard the sailboat.

Cole dropped his shoulders to add, "I should have been paying better attention."

"I told you I had it. I let you down," Whitney shot back immediately. She couldn't let him carry any of her own guilt. "I've never in my life made a mistake like that. I'll live with it for the rest of my life."

Cole didn't seem to know what to say. Whitney shuddered and turned her head all the way around, where the nurses had apparently put her phone on the nightstand. They'd even charged it.

Whitney reached for her phone, suddenly hopeful that her father had texted her back. She wasn't sure where the thought came from. Probably, she would have that hope for a long time.

Instead, she'd received an email from Kenny Baldwin's lawyer.

"Wow. He got on that fast," Whitney muttered as she scanned the email. The buzzwords were: "family in danger," "near-death experience," and "seeking an enormous settlement." Whitney read these words aloud to Cole, wincing.

"I'm not sure how I'll get out of this one," she said finally, throwing her phone back on the side table with regret. Her eyes filled with tears. "And it's not like I deserve to get out of it, either."

"Just because something bad happened to Kenny Baldwin doesn't mean he's not the world's biggest idiot," Cole shot back obstinately.

Whitney struggled to make herself smile. She wanted to do it if only to let Cole know how much she appreciated him.

But instead, she heard herself say the words she'd kept inside since last night.

"My dad just died."

What did she have to lose?

Immediately, Cole's smile fell to the floor. He stepped delicately toward the bed and placed his hand on her arm. Someone else's touch during a time of such intense horror and loneliness felt profound. Whitney blinked back tears.

Cole's own eyes filled with understanding. Already, he seemed to put two and two together. She hadn't been in her right mind, and mistakes had been made.

"Whitney. Your father is so proud of the person you are," Cole breathed.

Whitney shivered and cried, overwhelmed with how tragic it suddenly felt to say this truth aloud. Finally, she managed to say, "I can't believe I messed up so badly."

"You can't blame yourself for that," Cole told her softly. "You're a real, honest-to-goodness sailor. You've traveled around the world and know the seas better than anyone I've ever known. Yesterday was one of the worst days of your life. There's no denying that. And I won't be one of those people who says you'll get through this. People used to say that to me after my father died, and I wanted to laugh in their face and ask them, 'what makes you so sure?'"

A soft laugh rolled out of Whitney. She dug her head

Sailing Home

deeper into her pillow, suddenly overwhelmed with just how tired she felt. As Cole began to speak again, reminding her of all the things she was to him, she drifted back to sleep. It was a welcome relief from a world of so much pain.

Chapter Fourteen

That afternoon, the doctor at the hospital cleared Whitney to leave. He told her to manage her stress levels and her heart rate, avoid alcohol, and make sure to eat enough protein. Whitney half rolled her eyes during the doctor's speech and then stood on legs that seemed to shake beneath her. Cole stuck out his elbow, and she took it for support down the hallway.

"It looks like we're in a Jane Austen novel or something," Whitney teased herself. "Like you're courting me or something."

"Yeah. I'm after your dowry," Cole joked.

"Sorry to say that the dowry isn't much of anything at all," Whitney said, putting on a typical English accent.

"Wait." Cole stopped in the hallway and gave her a side-eye. "Was that really your English accent?"

"Cheerio, governor!" Whitney kept it going, her eyes flashing good-naturedly.

Cole's heart lifted as he snorted. "That is just about the worst English accent I've ever heard. If anyone from England ever hears that accent..."

Sailing Home

"What? What will they do?" Whitney demanded.

"You don't want to know," Cole told her. He shuddered purposely.

Whitney tossed her head back. Her laughter floated down the hallway like a song.

Outside, Cole hailed a cab, opened the back door of the vehicle, and watched as Whitney slid herself inside. Already, they'd booked two single rooms at a shoddy motel a few blocks from the dock. From there, they'd decide what to do next.

Once outside the doors of their hotel rooms, Whitney slid her key into the lock, bowed her head, and confessed, "I'm exhausted all over again. I think I'm going to sit in the air-conditioning, watch bad television, and crash."

"You want to grab dinner later?" Cole asked.

Whitney shrugged. "Maybe. If you get your phone back from the boat, text me. If I don't text back, I'm enjoying my sleep."

Cole laughed. "Fair enough. Take care of yourself, okay?"

* * *

Cole headed to the docks after check-in to chat with the harbor manager about the boat situation, collect his phone and other belongings, and inspect the damage to the boat. Whitney had told him that they needed to talk to the boat rental company she'd rented it from back in the British Virgin Islands, although she dreaded telling them what she'd done. "I definitely bought insurance," she'd said. "Although I'm sure I bought the cheapest insurance there was. I could be screwed."

The Great Escape had been lifted onto a trailer with

its mast tipped downward. The side of the hull was torn up pretty bad from the hit against the rock. Of this, the manager of the harbor laughed and said, "I can't believe you didn't go under." Then he asked, "Is it true that Whitney Silverton was the captain of the boat?"

To this question, Cole cocked his eyebrow and said, "Where did you hear that? Obviously, I was the one who was driving the boat. Do you see anyone named Whitney here?"

Cole's clear anger shut the man up quickly. Cole shifted the conversation, saying, "Thanks again for your help last night. I'm sorry. It's been a stressful twenty-four hours."

"I can imagine. That black eye alone tells me you haven't had it easy," the man said. "Where should I send the bill to?"

Cole gave him his email and phone number, deciding to talk to Whitney about it later. He then got onto the boat and searched the berth for his phone and other belongings. He also grabbed Whitney's bag, quickly shoving her T-shirts and shorts into it and zipping it tight.

That night, Cole sat at the edge of his bed in the motel. There was a dip in the middle, proof that thousands upon thousands of other lonely guys had slept in the same bed. He sent Whitney a text to see if she wanted to eat dinner, but after thirty-five minutes without a response, Cole reasoned that she was still fast asleep or wanted to be left alone.

Cole headed out and grabbed himself a chicken sandwich from a fast food place. It wasn't typical Caribbean food, and that, for Cole, was the point. As he sat with grease dripping off his fingers, he ached with nostalgia

Sailing Home

and homesickness. *Why was he so far away from Martha's Vineyard with his heart in his throat?*

As he chewed through his second leg of chicken, a phone call rang through from none other than Elsa Remington, Cole's mother. Cole answered before it got to the second ring.

"Hi!" He sounded like a little kid.

"Well, hello, Cole Steel." He could hear that she was smiling. "I'm surprised you can talk."

"You hit me at a good time," Cole told her.

"That's good to hear! Where are you in the world?"

Cole stared down at the grease-laden chicken and the platter of french fries he'd ordered at the last second. His skin was red from the sun, his stomach felt sick, and his head still pounded from Garrett's punch. The black eye looked insane on him like he was a pirate with a natural eyepatch.

"I'm in Grenada," Cole told her. "And, um, I have some news."

"Oh?" Elsa's voice tinged with worry.

"Yeah." Cole dropped his shoulders and tried to tell himself that this wasn't giving up. "There was an accident on the boat."

"Oh my God! Are you okay?" Elsa sounded terrified.

"It's okay. Really. I'm fine. I just have a little concussion."

Did he? Maybe. He probably should have been checked by the doctor.

"A concussion? Oh, Cole. I hope you're not sleeping?"

"I'm okay. Really." Cole was aware that he hadn't fully answered her question. "I just want to come home for a little while, if that's okay."

Cole closed his eyes, genuinely surprised that he'd allowed himself to say what he actually wanted. For two months, he'd pushed himself into this life in the Caribbean, praying it would get better. Each day had been a struggle. Now, he sat in a chicken place with a black eye, his vessel had some pretty epic holes in it, and he had nowhere to call home.

"Honey. You know that you can come home whenever you want," Elsa whispered. "You're always welcome here."

"I just don't want it to seem like I gave up."

He was surprised he said those words aloud, too.

"You're not giving up," Elsa countered, although she had to say that. She was his mother. "You're giving your body some much-needed rest. And nutrition, too. I'll start making some clam chowder this second."

That night, Cole slept fitfully. His emotions alternated between fear that he'd made the wrong decision and relief he was headed home. He wasn't sure how he would explain this to Whitney. *Where would she wind up when all of this was over?* The Kenny Baldwin legal case was only just beginning. *Would she have the strength to withstand whatever chaos he threw at her? Would she just jump on her own sailboat and run away?*

The following morning, Whitney texted Cole back.

> WHITNEY: I slept another twenty hours. Pretty insane that my body allows me to do that.
>
> WHITNEY: What are your plans today?

> COLE: I'm headed out now to pick up a rental truck. The plan is to drive the boat over to the repairman and chat about what's next.

> WHITNEY: Thanks for doing that. Seriously. You're a lifesaver.

> WHITNEY: I guess I'll be an "adult" and call the boat rental company and see what they say about the accident. Time to face the music.

> COLE: Maybe we can meet up tonight for dinner?

> WHITNEY: I'll see how I feel.

The boat repairman reminded Cole a lot of the manager of the Grenada Harbor. He had broad shoulders and a sagging gut and seemed eager to ask questions about who else had been on the boat with Cole because "he'd heard rumors." Cole did his best to squash those rumors. He didn't want Whitney's legacy to be tainted.

After he spoke to the repairman about the amount of time he probably needed to "fix her up," Cole wandered along the boardwalk with his hands shoved in his pockets. Across the horizon, boats skidded across the waves, their sails flashing in the wind. Just then, Cole felt utterly landlocked. His sailboat remained back in the British Virgin Islands. He ached for it; he ached for anything related to sailing and the ocean.

Where he walked, ritzy hotels staggered across the boardwalk and the beaches. Turquoise pools glinted out front, stretching up toward state-of-the-art bars, which allowed a bartender to serve you even as you stayed in the water. Cole had never been to a resort like that. Being a sailing and beer guy, he wasn't sure he'd like it.

Suddenly, a beautiful voice rang out like a song.

"Cole?"

Cole stopped and turned back.

It was Aria.

She stood in an army-green dress with a fluttering skirt, and her hair was just as wild as ever, the blond coils running off toward the sun. Her big eyes took in every inch of him.

"Oh. Hi." Cole eyed the resorts along the water, putting two and two together. When the Baldwins had stalked off the sailboat, he'd put them out of his mind. Obviously, they'd just hopped into the nearest state-of-the-art hotel and decided to have a different kind of vacation.

"Cole, I..." Aria took a delicate step toward him. Her eyes were heavy with tears. "I'm so happy I ran into you."

Cole remained silent. Anger was the only thing he understood just then.

"I'm just so, so sorry for what my father did on that boat," she rasped. "I hope that your eye wasn't..."

"No. Your father didn't punch me. Although I'm sure he really wanted to."

Aria dropped her eyes to the ground, heavy with shame. For a moment, Cole regretted it before shoving that away. There just wasn't time for regret.

"Yesterday was just terrible," she whispered. "When he turned on you like that, I had no idea what to do. He was so drunk. Everyone was drunk."

Cole wanted to tell her that she should have stayed away from him, especially when it was clear that her father didn't like them together. *But wasn't that hypocriti-*

Sailing Home

cal? It was true that they'd done nothing but chat. Her father had blown the whole thing out of proportion.

"It's hard to explain," Aria continued, stepping closer so she could lower her voice. "My father has always wanted me to behave like my brother and sister. He's wanted me to marry someone successful and have little babies and live my life as a good and behaved Baldwin. In his eyes, I almost made it because I was engaged to Benjamin Bottom of the very rich Bottom family."

Aria couldn't help it; she snorted as she said his full name.

Cole allowed himself to smile for only a moment.

"It's not about the name," Aria protested. "I would be a Mrs. Bottom if Mr. Bottom was a brilliant and kind and wonderful individual. But in this case, well. Benjamin Bottom was nothing if not cruel, manipulative, and selfish. Much like the rest of my family. No wonder they liked him."

Aria's cheeks were blotchy with embarrassment. "I left Ben last year and stopped talking to my family. Recently, they won me back. I thought I could make it work, that I could forgive them. But this trip showed me that they'll never change."

Cole nodded. "Sometimes, you have to listen to your gut."

"Always," Aria offered.

They held the silence for a long time. Aria stuttered as she asked, "What's next for you?"

Cole wasn't sure he wanted to tell her. He wanted to divide his life into a "before" and an "after" and never really think of the Baldwins again.

But instead, he said, "I'm listening to my gut and returning home. Martha's Vineyard is the place for me right now. I need to rest and nurse myself back to health, both mentally and physically."

Aria nodded knowingly. "If you have people to go back to, people who you love and who love you? That's the greatest gift in the world. You can't squander that."

Again, silence. The water rushed up along the beach and then retreated into the enormity of what it truly was. Cole wondered why humans dared to mess around with the ocean in the first place.

"And what will Whitney do?" Aria asked softly.

Cole's heart thudded. He wished for an answer but came up with nothing. "Whitney Silverton always lands on her feet."

He wasn't sure if this was true this time around.

"I have to go," Cole told Aria, his voice firm. "I wish you well, with or without your family. I hope we both learn to trust our gut and actually listen to it."

Aria looked as though she wanted to rush toward him and hug him. Cole kept his body stiff and turned back just before she could.

Aria called out, "Goodbye, Cole Steel." He just waved a hand as he walked away.

Cole felt delirious as he walked away from her, his tongue scratchy like sandpaper. He still sensed that Aria's eyes were on his back, but when he turned around, he saw no one but strangers.

Suddenly, he had his phone in his hand. A call rang out across the Caribbean Sea and up the Atlantic coastline, all the way to Martha's Vineyard.

When Elsa answered on the second ring, Cole realized just how much worry she'd been stewing in since he'd asked to come home.

"Honey? Are you all right?"

Sailing Home

"Yeah. Yeah. I'm fine." Cole swallowed. "I just have a request."

"Anything, Cole. You know that."

Cole's heart pounded. "I wondered if you might have a space at the Lodge any time soon? I have a dear friend who might need some time and space away from real life for a little while. She's suffered a number of losses lately, and I don't think it'll be easy for her to get back on her feet. I know that you, Nancy, Aunt Carmella, and Aunt Janine are the ones to help her."

"Oh, honey." Elsa's voice quivered. "Send her our way. We'll do all we can."

Chapter Fifteen

Tyson Silverton's funeral was held in Miami on the fifth of October. It was yet another sweltering day, a humid ninety-one degrees. It was the kind of heat that sucked the personality out of your body, the kind that made your hair stick to your neck and your heart beat slower. Down in the Caribbean, such horrific heat spells were rare. When they came, Whitney only had to leap into the Caribbean Sea to get away from it all.

Those days were over now.

Whitney awoke in yet another cigarette-smelling motel room on the outskirts of Miami. She hadn't wanted to stay at her father and Liz's place without her father around; had she asked if she could crash on the couch, she was pretty sure Liz would have said no, anyway. Fearful of approaching legal fees and where she would ever get money again, a motel room had been her only answer. Gosh, she was tired of them.

In the shower, Whitney stood in lukewarm water and stared into space. The past five days or so had been a

Sailing Home

whirlwind, and it was hard to tell her mind and heart to calm down enough to handle the weight of this horrific day. She wished she could press fast-forward and get it all over with.

Just three days ago, she and Cole had hugged at the Maurice Bishop International Airport, where he'd told her his idea. "My grandfather started a health lodge, where people from all over the world come to rest up and heal after traumatic events."

"Uh?" she'd said, not sure where he was headed with that.

Cole had shrugged and said, "I talked to my mom about it, and she says there's a place for you there if you want it. Free of charge."

To this, Whitney had laughed. "I don't need health and wellness, Cole. I just need some time alone."

They'd hugged again. Cole had called her stubborn and said he would miss her.

After that, Whitney had taken a plane to the British Virgin Islands. There, she'd met with the boat rental company and explained the extent of the damage on their boat and shown photographs. Afterward, they'd arranged for another sailor to bring the boat up from Grenada after the boat itself was fully operational. This, of course, would come out of Whitney's pocket. The insurance hadn't been anything to write home about.

During this meeting, the rental company manager had looked her dead in the eye and asked, "What the heck happened out there, Whitney?"

That question seemed to appear around every corner, especially across the British Virgin Islands. Her father's friends, in particular, seemed at a loss and curious for answers. Whitney wanted to tell them that Tyson had just died, that she was in mourning, that she couldn't talk about the accident if she tried.

When the time came, though, she couldn't bring herself to tell his friends about Tyson's death. As far as many of Tyson's old friends knew, Tyson was still alive. She almost liked it better that way. He lived on in spirit in the Caribbean.

After her shower, Whitney brushed her hair and wrapped it up in a towel. She then tugged a black dress out of her backpack and assessed the wrinkles. They were deep and angry, proof that they had lived in the back of her sailboat's closet for what seemed like years. The last funeral she'd attended had been for Garrett's Great-Aunt Margaret. After the funeral, Garrett had gotten into a massive argument with his mother and tugged Whitney out of there. Yet another red flag Whitney had chosen not to see.

The motel had the world's oldest-looking iron and ironing board. Whitney nearly chopped off a finger as she unfurled the board. The squeak as she opened it nearly cut her eardrum in two.

The iron worked. As Whitney pulled the iron over the wrinkles, she imagined herself like a 1950s housewife, preparing her husband for work. *Had those women felt loved and protected? Had they felt like they belonged? Or had they felt used each time they ironed their husbands' shirts?* It was difficult for Whitney to imagine either course. Garrett had never once needed a shirt to be ironed. Maybe, at one time, she would have liked to demonstrate her love in that way.

Whitney was dressed and ready for the funeral a good three hours before it was set to begin. This wasn't like her. To kill time, she wandered down to the docks to watch the

Sailing Home

boats. It was a force of habit, she supposed. Also, she wanted to assess how she felt when she looked at them. She hadn't been on a boat at all since the accident, save for jumping onto her sailboat back in the British Virgin Islands to grab a bag of her things. That was how she'd gotten the black dress.

The idea of sailing out into the wide-open blue terrified her.

It had never terrified her before.

Whitney hovered at the edge of the docks. This close to the water, a breeze sliced through the thick humidity and felt cool against the sweat that bubbled along her cheeks and forehead. Across the water, sailors curled their ropes around their elbows and chatted with neighboring boats. From what Whitney could hear, most everyone wanted to talk about the weather or where they were sailing next. Whitney remembered those simple conversations. They were ones she'd had in harbors all across the world.

"Excuse me?" A man's voice came from her left.

Whitney turned to find a man in his forties or fifties with salt-and-pepper hair and a confident smile. He looked like a banker or a business owner. There was no mistaking that he spoke to her.

"Hi?"

Beside the man, a little girl held his hand and swung it around anxiously. She wore a pair of overalls much like the ones Whitney had worn as a girl. Actually, she'd lived in her overalls from the age of four onward.

"You wouldn't happen to be Whitney Silverton, would you?" the man asked.

Whitney's heart pounded. It was strange to hear her

name so far from the harbors she truly knew down in the Caribbean.

"She is, Daddy!" the little girl whispered. She didn't think Whitney could hear her.

Whitney forced herself to smile. The little girl looked at her like she was the sun, the moon, and the stars put together. Whitney wasn't accustomed to that.

"I'm Whitney Silverton," she said, mostly to the girl. "And what are your names?"

"I'm Ricki!" the little girl squealed. "This is my dad!"

Whitney's heart cracked. "Hi, Ricki and Ricki's dad."

"That is my legal name," the man said with a laugh.

Ricki stepped behind her father's leg and peered around it, suddenly embarrassed. The man said, "She's starstruck. We followed several of your races over the past couple of years. You were such a godsend for me, you know?"

Whitney couldn't imagine being a godsend for anyone. She looked at him incredulously.

"I wanted to get Ricki into sailing," the man explained. "But sailing is such a boy's club. When you appeared on the cover of *World Sailing Magazine* two years back, Ricki could hardly believe it. The next day, I had her out on the boat with me. She's been captivated with sailing and with your career ever since."

Whitney's eyes filled with tears. *Don't cry in front of this marvelous little girl. Don't show her just how emotional you actually are. She has to believe in something, and for some reason, she's chosen to believe in you.*

Whitney bent down to make eye contact with Ricki. "You must be very talented at sailing, Ricki."

Ricki nodded slightly. Her eyes told Whitney a story of confidence.

Sailing Home

"Which boat is yours?" The man searched across the harbor expectantly. Probably, he'd seen a photograph of Whitney's boat in that very magazine article. Whitney had decked it out, making it state of the art and uniquely hers.

"Oh. Um." How could she say she'd left her boat back in the British Virgin Islands? That her father had died? That she wasn't sure she would ever sail again. "It's over there." She pointed a finger off to the left.

Both Ricki and her father craned to see where Whitney pointed. This was her cue to exit. She turned on a heel and called out, "I have to run. It was great to meet you. Happy sailing, Ricki!"

By the time she walked to the funeral home, her black dress stuck to her back, and her legs were dewy with sweat. Outside the small, squat funeral home, Liz stood in a black dress and a pair of sensible heels and spoke with another woman in her sixties or seventies. Whitney emerged from the sidewalk feeling like the *Creature from the Black Lagoon*. Liz hardly registered her.

"Liz?" Whitney stood a few feet away from her stepmother.

Liz glanced Whitney's way, her eyes shimmering with annoyance. "Oh! It's you." She didn't sound pleased. "Melanie, this is Tyson's daughter. Oh. Gosh, Whitney. You should really clean up inside."

Whitney glanced toward the friend, who looked at Whitney with a mix of interest and disgust. Liz didn't bother to reach out to hug Whitney. They were like perfect strangers.

"Okay. Well. I'll see you in there?"

Liz sniffed as Whitney moved past. There was silence behind her for a long time until, right when Whitney reached the door, she thought she could hear Liz say, "You won't believe the kind of woman she is."

Whitney didn't care to wait around to learn the answer to that.

The inside of the funeral home was musty with the smell of flowers. It was incredible, really, that the smell seemed so unnatural. *Hadn't these people ever run through a field of flowers before? Hadn't they ever bent to smell lavender?* Whitney and her father certainly had. Any time Whitney had discovered flowers on their multiple adventures, she'd bent to pick him a bouquet. He'd always decorated their little table on the sailboat with flowers. They'd sat so proudly in their vase.

The bathroom mirror reflected back a woman on the verge of a mental breakdown. Her makeup had run down her cheeks and around her eyes, and her lipstick had bludgeoned her chin. Her hair stuck to her back and neck, and her black dress, despite being black, was still blotchy with sweat. Whitney dropped her head directly beneath the faucet and turned the water on as cold as she could. It was still only lukewarm.

Without her makeup on, the wrinkles on her forty-three-year-old face made the skin beneath her eyes look like crepe paper. Her cheeks looked hollowed out, and her lips looked lifeless. Her purse offered very few solutions. She had some purple lipstick for some reason, plus some sunscreen. She added the sunscreen and fluffed her hair, lifting her eyes to the ceiling. It wasn't like anyone she cared about would see her there, anyway. Her dad was gone.

Tyson had requested to be cremated, which felt a bit sad for Whitney. She'd wanted to see his face one last time, no matter how "off" it had become in death.

Sailing Home

Instead, she wandered through the funeral halls and gazed at the photographs that Liz had arranged. Most of them had been taken in the years after Tyson and Liz had met and fallen in love. There were photos of them on cruise ships (which was insane, as Tyson had always detested cruise ships), in front of the Colosseum in Rome, cozying up at home on the couch, and sunning at the beach. Multiple other friends appeared in the photographs, proof that Tyson had enjoyed a very social life during his last decades.

It was entirely unlike the life he'd had out at sea with his daughter.

Had he been happier after he'd left the Caribbean? It was a question that would haunt Whitney for the rest of her life.

Whitney grabbed a seat in the third row of the grand hall, watching as other mourners arrived to pay their respects. She recognized several of them from the photographs. They dabbed the corners of their eyes with handkerchiefs and spoke in soft tones that Liz couldn't understand. None of them looked like "sailing types." *What had they done together? Played cards? Barbecued? Did they know about Tyson's vagabond daughter? Did they know him at all?*

The service began. Liz's pastor approached the pulpit and spoke eloquently about the first time he'd ever met Tyson, who'd been a self-described nonbeliever at the time. "It was a beautiful thing, watching him join our church and learn the scripture," the pastor continued.

Whitney's heart ballooned. She hadn't known that her father joined the church. She glanced toward the ceiling, suddenly awash with ideas of heaven. Although she'd hardly studied the Bible herself, the idea of him up there somewhere in the clouds did give her a bit of hope.

The hope didn't last.

After the pastor, one after another of Tyson's friends approached the pulpit, each with stories about Tyson Silverton. Whitney, who'd heard nearly every story about her father out at sea, had never heard any of these stories. Her eyes became glossy; her chin wiggled, threatening to destroy her.

The stories were mundane; there was no doubt about that. Still, they breathed life into the man who'd left her behind in the Caribbean. They breathed life into the man who was now long gone.

After the sixth speech, Whitney found herself on her feet. The strangers around her gaped as she approached the pulpit, waving a hand as if to say, *don't worry. I got this.* But what exactly was she doing? Nobody had asked her to speak. Nobody at the funeral knew who she was at all.

The pastor had arrived at the pulpit to give a final blessing. He tilted his head as Whitney approached.

"Did you want to say a few words?" He sounded kind, if confused.

"I know I'm not on the pamphlet." Whitney shrugged. "I won't be long."

"Of course." The pastor stepped back and gestured forward so that Whitney could take his space.

Whitney found herself standing in front of what looked to be two hundred mourners. All two hundred pairs of eyes were heavy with confusion. *Who was this woman? And why wasn't she wearing any makeup?*

"Hi." Whitney rasped into the microphone.

In the front row, Liz glowered at her. Whitney forced

Sailing Home

her eyes away, unwilling to think twice about the woman. This wasn't about her.

"You probably don't know me," Whitney continued. "But Tyson Silverton was my father. And I'd like to say something about our time together."

Whispers rushed through the crowd like wildfires.

"My mother left when I was a baby," Whitney began, her voice wavering. "Unlike most little girls, I never cared about where my mother was or why she'd left us behind. I had my father. He was my entire world. I grew up on his sailboat, which he called *Laura* after his mother, my grandmother. We went all over the world together. He taught me everything I know."

Whitney's eyes filled with tears, so much so that the people in the crowd before her were just blotches of colors. She liked them better this way.

"This one time, we were sailing along the eastern coastline of South America," Whitney said. "And Dad pointed out across the water and said, 'Look, Whitney! It's a Great White Shark!' I was ecstatic to see one because I'd pored over *National Geographic* magazines and knew everything there was to know about sharks. I wasn't afraid. We watched the shark swim out toward deeper waters, and my dad told me that all great white sharks swim alone. I laughed at him. What a silly guy, I thought! Because I remembered from my magazines that great whites don't always swim alone. They often swim in pairs or packs and help each other."

Here, Whitney's voice broke. She blinked, and a single tear slid down her cheek.

"He said, 'I guess that makes us great white sharks, Bug,'" Whitney continued, losing steam. "'Because we both need each other a whole lot more than we think we do. And that's a fact.'"

Whitney puffed her cheeks full of air. Across the funeral home, silence swelled and grew as thick as the humidity outside. A million other stories came to the surface of her mind, but none of them seemed good enough. Even this great white shark story seemed lifeless compared to how much she loved her father.

"Anyway." Whitney had gotten too close to the microphone, and the voice was painfully loud. Liz snapped her hands over her ears.

Whitney staggered back, overwhelmed. She locked eyes with one of the photographs on the far wall, in which her father gave one of his secretive smiles. *How was it possible that she'd never see him again? What on earth would she become without him?*

Whitney rushed down the aisle. Around her, the mourners whispered wildly, probably thrilled at the spectacle.

Whitney shoved herself through the front door of the funeral home, cupped her knees, and gasped for air. Across the street, a woman tried to parallel park in a spot that seemed too small for her car. It was funny how the world just went on without you.

She wandered down the road with no direction in mind. Eventually, the woman gave up on her parallel parking job and raced down the street, her tires squealing. Whitney tried to focus on her breathing, but her anxiety seemed to spike regardless.

When she reached an intersection she didn't recognize, Whitney grabbed her phone to check out a map. Instead of opening up the map functionality, however, she found herself dialing a familiar number.

"Whitney!" Cole sounded happier than he'd been at the Grenada Airport. Whitney could practically feel the sun on his face and the home-cooked meals in his belly.

"Hi, Cole."

"Is today the funeral?"

"It just finished." Whitney's heart pounded.

"God, I'm sorry. I'm so sorry you're going through that alone. Nobody should have to." The thing about Cole was that you believed him when he said stuff like that. He actually meant it.

"Yeah." Whitney cleared her throat.

"Where are you now?" Cole asked.

Whitney stared at a turning sign that advertised a fast food restaurant. "I think I need to come to Martha's Vineyard."

Her mind roared with what she really wanted to say—that she needed out of the horrible heat of Miami. That she needed to get as far away from Liz as she could. That she couldn't go back to the British Virgin Islands and face all those questions about the accident.

Cole seemed to know that questions weren't important just then. "You have a room whenever you want it. I promised you that."

Chapter Sixteen

The bay window of Whitney's suite fogged against the chill of the early October morning. Whitney sat in a fuzzy robe the Katama Lodge had given her, her legs crossed as she traced a line through the fog of the window and peered out at the gray waters of Katama Bay. She felt terribly far from any world she understood. Perhaps that was for the best.

It was Saturday, her first full day on Martha's Vineyard. The previous three days had passed in a frenzy of responsibilities, gut-wrenching phone calls, and a plane ride up to Boston, during which she'd wept quietly the entire time.

Now, her boat in the British Virgin Islands had been removed from the water and stored in a warehouse that belonged to an old friend of her father's. She'd notified her lawyer of her whereabouts at the Katama Lodge, where he would send any official documentation regarding the upcoming legal battle with Kenny Baldwin. She'd even texted Liz where she was off to, although Liz hadn't bothered to respond. Whitney's spontaneous

Sailing Home

speech at the funeral hadn't been well-received. That was putting it lightly.

Each suite at the Katama Lodge came with a small kitchenette with coffee, tea, fresh fruits, fresh bread, jam, and peanut butter. Whitney heated water and placed a green tea bag in a mug. As her anxiety had been through the roof since the day her father died, she didn't need the heart-bursting effects of coffee. Besides, she was at the Katama Lodge to heal, wasn't she? That meant paying attention to what her body was telling her. Or something like that.

Whitney sat again at the bay window and sipped the steaming tea. Off to the right, her schedule for the next few days sat as a reminder. Saturday and Sunday were her days to settle in. Monday morning began with yoga, followed by a healthy breakfast at the Lodge cafeteria. After that, she would meet with Janine Grimson, a naturopathic doctor. Together, apparently, they would create a strategy to align Whitney's heart, mind, spirit, and body. Whitney wasn't sure what that meant, but it sounded worth a shot.

The previous afternoon, Cole had picked Whitney up at the Boston Logan International Airport. Behind the wheel of his beat-up pickup truck, he had told her that she would probably think the Katama Lodge was "a lot of hippie stuff."

"But I can't tell you the number of women who've stayed at the Lodge. Many of them have written my mother, my aunts, or my stepgrandmother, saying how beneficial their time at the Lodge was. Before my grandfather died, he kept a big stack of those letters in his office. He told me that if I could help just one person during my time on earth, I had to do it."

Whitney had held the silence for a moment, watching the ominous clouds outside the truck window. Boston was a far different beast than her normal world in the Caribbean.

"You're telling me that I have to give it a chance, even if I'm not feeling it?" Whitney had finally asked, giving Cole a secret smile.

"Something like that," Cole said.

After that, Cole had driven his pickup directly onto the ferry in Woods Hole, Massachusetts. Whitney had remained in the dark of the belly of the ferry, her eyes closed. Unlike sailing, the ferry seemed sturdy in the water, so much so that she could almost pretend she was back on land. Almost.

Cole had sat with her, wordless. It was probably remarkable and terrifying to see the "great" Whitney Silverton like that. Bless him, he didn't say a thing about it.

Whitney continued to sip her green tea that Saturday morning, her heart thudding slowly. Cole shouldn't have been worried about her "giving the Lodge a chance." It wasn't like she had anywhere else to go in the world. This was it.

A knock sounded on the door. Whitney tilted her head, unsure, initially, if the knock had been at her door or another's. But a few seconds later, a timid voice called out, "Whitney? Are you up?"

Whitney tiptoed toward the door and opened it just a crack. It was the woman from the sailing regatta several weeks ago. Cole's mother. Her smile was slightly earnest yet filled with hope.

"Good morning!" The woman greeted her with a smile. "I wanted to properly introduce myself and

Sailing Home

welcome you to the Katama Lodge and Wellness Spa. I apologize that I wasn't here to greet you yesterday. My grandson had a doctor's appointment, and I offered to take him. My daughter has been pressed for time lately..."

Whitney blinked out at her, overwhelmed.

"Oh, gosh. I'm sorry." The woman waved her hand over her face. "Sometimes, when I get started talking, I just go and go. Cole probably warned you about that."

Whitney tried to smile. "He only said wonderful things about you."

The woman's cheeks burned pink. After a dramatic pause, she burst out with, "I can't thank you enough for protecting him out on the water. That accident must have been rough. Cole's black eye has finally started to go down a little bit, thank goodness."

Whitney speculated that Cole hadn't told his mother very much about the actual accident. He'd certainly left Garrett out of the story altogether, thankfully.

"It was a scary time," Whitney affirmed. "We wouldn't have gotten out of it without him."

The woman's eyes glittered with tears. Whitney's stomach twisted with anxiety. Finally, Whitney said, "I'm really sorry. I don't think I ever learned your name."

"Oh! I'm Elsa." Elsa shook her head to wade off the tears. "I guess you wouldn't want to call me 'Cole's Mom' for the rest of your stay."

"Ha. No. That wouldn't work." Whitney realized her own smile felt genuine. This woman had all the same goodness as Cole, just packaged up differently. "Thank you again for letting me stay here. The room is spectacular."

Elsa peeked behind Whitney. "When Cole said you needed the space, I knew we had to make it happen."

"It'll only be for a little while," Whitney said, lifting her chin.

But Elsa locked eyes with her. "You take as long as you need." She paused and then added, "I lost my father last year and my husband a few years back. I can't tell you how lost I was. I hope that this place that my father built becomes a refuge for you."

Whitney nodded, at a loss for what to say.

"By the way," Elsa added, her words quick to take over the silence between them. "We're having a family get-together this afternoon at my place. It's just about a mile west down the beach, a big place with a sign out front that says 'Remington.' Would you be interested in joining us? I know that the rest of the family would love to meet you."

Whitney's heartbeat quickened. *A family get-together?* Images flashed through her mind— of picnics, laughing faces, someone blowing out the candles on a birthday cake. This wasn't a world she understood. She would stick out like a bump on a log.

"Oh. Um." Whitney shook her head, at a loss.

"You can think about it," Elsa said. "We won't get started till around two. Take the morning to settle in and pop over if you feel up to it."

"Sure. Thank you." Whitney thought the likelihood of her "popping over" was about zero. She was grateful for the invitation, anyway.

* * *

Sailing Home

Whitney spent the morning latched away in her suite. In the hallway, she could hear the other Katama Lodge residents chatting easily and saying things like, "We should really go into town and walk along the boardwalk," or, "Want to grab a green juice downstairs?" Whitney couldn't imagine making a friend. *What were the mechanics of something like that?* Most women at the Lodge would probably sense something "off" about Whitney.

Yes, Whitney had "made friends" with Cole. *But did that count?* She'd technically hired him. Now, he'd taken pity on her and arranged for a free spot in his mother's health clinic. That wasn't exactly friendship.

Whitney showered and inspected each of the lavender-scented soaps. Someone had selected them purposely to create the Katama Lodge ambiance. Whitney used them in small portions, thinking she could take the leftovers with her wherever she went next. A lifetime of generic shampoo and soap made luxurious soaps seem otherworldly.

Once outside the shower, Whitney sat in front of an antique circular mirror and decided, for the first time in quite a while, to brush her hair. When she let it tangle for days on end, it was a clear sign that her depression had returned. Here it was, back with a vengeance.

It took her more than thirty minutes to get all the tangles out. The brush filled with her red hair and several white and gray ones.

Around one, Whitney forced herself outside to walk the grounds of the Lodge. Katama Bay lapped across the beach, reflecting back the gray October clouds above. The biting chill to the air proved that Whitney was far, far away from that thick Miami air. It was easy to breathe, but it also made Whitney feel like curling up in bed and hiding from the world.

"Just go to their party," Whitney muttered to herself, suddenly annoyed. "They're going out of their way to help you for free, for goodness' sake. It wouldn't kill you to show up, eat a slice of cake or whatever, and then head out. Make an appearance, then get back in bed."

Whitney rolled her eyes inwardly at her own stupidity. She then kicked her feet through the sand, gave the Katama Bay a rueful glare, then headed westward down the beach. Elsa had said about a mile, with a big sign out front. "Remington."

It was one thing to have a place to call home. It was another to be so gosh-darn proud of that place that you labeled it like that.

The walk toward the Remington House was internal and achy. Whitney caught herself watching the white-capped waves as they frothed across the Atlantic. Seagulls cawed overhead, their tone slightly different than in the Caribbean. Whitney tugged the zipper of her sweatshirt all the way to her chin and shivered. It was probably only about fifty-five degrees.

By the time she reached the sign that read "Remington," Whitney had nearly convinced herself to return to the Katama Lodge. *What on earth could she offer these people except her own busted-up heart?* She lifted her eyes to the beautiful home along the water, with its wrap-around porch and its glowing windows. Several cars were parked in the driveway and along the road. *Should she have brought something? A bottle of wine? A box of cookies?*

Suddenly, the front door burst open to reveal Elsa. She waved and called out, "Whitney! I thought that was you. Come on in! We have a glass of wine with your name on it."

Whitney shoved her hands in the pockets of her sweatshirt and forced her legs forward. *Was she smiling?* She couldn't feel her cheeks due to the cold. Each step up the porch felt like a mountain.

"It's chilly out here," Elsa said as she led her into the foyer. "You should have called Cole and made him pick you up."

Whitney's laughter sounded unnatural. "I needed the walk." Her eyes scanned the foyer and the immediate next room, where several people sat on couches with glasses of wine or cans of beer. The rooms were decorated with beautiful antiques, each with a remarkable personality.

Elsa introduced everyone in the first living room. "This is my sister, Carmella, and her husband, Cody."

When Whitney stepped closer to shake Carmella's hand, she realized that Carmella was pregnant. This was a surprise. If Whitney wasn't mistaken, Carmella was around Whitney's age. It was a rare thing to see pregnant women in their forties.

"Lovely to meet you, Whitney," Carmella said. "I'll see you around the Lodge this week, I hope? I'm the acupuncturist."

"Ah!" Acupuncture was another thing that Whitney thought was a little "hippie-dippy," but she didn't let it show. "I can't wait to try it out."

"You'll love it," Carmella offered.

The others in the living room were introduced next. Bruce Holland had been on the docks in the British Virgin Islands but was now introduced as Elsa's boyfriend. A young woman named Alyssa carried a toddler named Lucy, bobbing her to distract her from her grumpiness.

"You're such an epic sailor," Alyssa told her, wide-eyed. "Cole is in awe of you."

"Oh, I..." Whitney wasn't sure what to say. "I'm in awe of Cole, too."

"Cole, did you hear that?" Alyssa called.

A split second later, Cole appeared in the living room with a glass of wine and a can of beer. He passed the glass off to Whitney and said, "Don't listen to anything my cousin says."

Whitney had to smile at this version of Cole, so different from the version she'd lived with onboard a boat for a couple of weeks. His black eye looked a great deal better, and he wore a clean-cut T-shirt and a pair of slacks. You could tell he was the kind of guy who dressed up to please his mother.

"How's your room?" Cole asked Whitney.

"Oh. It's lovely." Whitney surprised herself with how genuine she sounded. "Really. I feel like I can finally think."

She wasn't sure thinking was a good thing. Still, it was far and away better than any motel room.

"I'm glad to hear that," Cole said, palming the back of his neck. "I just signed a three-month lease at the little apartment complex I was living in before I left for the Caribbean. I figure three months will give me enough time to figure out what's next."

Whitney's heart jumped. She hadn't imagined that Cole would sign a lease. She'd thought this was a temporary "rest" for Cole before he got back out into the sailing world.

Sailing Home

"And I've already started giving lessons again at the Edgartown Sailing Club," he continued.

"Wow. You're really back."

Cole shrugged and glanced around the room. His family had burst into multiple conversations. Laughter echoed from wall to wall.

"Come on," Elsa said suddenly, stepping toward Whitney. "I want you to meet my stepmother, Nancy."

Whitney followed Elsa into the kitchen, where she met Nancy and Elsa's daughter, Mallory. Mallory's son sat in a highchair and swatted his plastic spoon against the table in front of him. Both Mallory and Nancy greeted Whitney joyfully. Nancy insisted Whitney eat one of her peanut butter oatmeal cookies and tell her if it was "good enough." Whitney couldn't have imagined a more delectable cookie.

"Sit down, Whitney," Nancy instructed as she dried her hands on a kitchen towel. "And tell us everything about yourself."

"Oh, don't put so much pressure on her," Elsa insisted.

"Are you interrogating someone, Mom?" Another woman popped into the kitchen. She eyed Whitney curiously and said, "You must be Whitney Silverton. My name is Janine."

"Oh!" Whitney remembered the name from the schedule. "You're my doctor."

Janine laughed. "Not today." She pressed a finger to her lips and poured herself a glass of wine. "Mom, instead of bothering Whitney, why don't we get started on dinner?"

"I was not bothering her," Nancy insisted with a wry smile. "Was I, Whitney?"

"I know how she can be," Janine teased. "She's so nosy. We can hardly let her out of the house."

Whitney settled into the chair across from Zachery, nibbled on her oatmeal cookie, sipped her wine, and allowed herself to fall into the bubbling conversation. It felt as though she'd stepped into a sitcom, one where everyone squabbled and bickered yet always came together at the end of the day to help each other out. *What character did she play in their sitcom? Was she the newcomer? Or the character who just passed through town on her way someplace else?*

The day continued on much as it had begun. Alyssa's sister, Maggie, soon appeared with her husband, Rex. Maggie sat with Whitney for a little while and talked about all things Brooklyn, which nearly bored Whitney to tears. Alyssa burst in and livened up the conversation a bit, talking about how they'd come to care for the little girl, Lucy. This was far more fascinating than Brooklyn real estate prices.

Around the table on the back porch, enclosed against the afternoon's chill, Nancy led the family in prayer and then ordered them to "eat to their heart's content." Whitney spooned a large amount of clam chowder across her tongue and closed her eyes as waves of flavor fell over her. This was truly spectacular.

When she opened her eyes, she found Elsa peering across the table at her. "What do you think?" she asked.

"It's extraordinary," Whitney breathed.

Elsa nodded knowingly. "A family recipe. Passed down from generation to generation."

"When are you planning on passing that recipe along to one of us?" Mallory asked her mother.

Sailing Home

"When I decide you're ready," Elsa said mischievously.

Cole laughed uproariously. Whitney snickered as well and took another bite of clam chowder. Nancy commented on the thick clouds overhead. "It's official. No more warm days from here on out. Not till spring."

Whitney spoke sparingly over the course of the afternoon and early evening. Sometimes, she found it incredibly shocking that she remained at the Remington House at all. Other times, she recognized it as the perfect distraction from her own broken heart. Occasionally, people asked her questions about her background, but more often than not, they were content that she sat with them, that she listened and ate the food they'd prepared. She drank two glasses of wine and then another and soon found her own laughter, which bubbled along with the others.

She wasn't happy; in fact, she was far from it. But gosh, it was great to just pretend for a little while— that she had this life and this family.

"Thank you for this," Whitney whispered to Cole in the hallway as they passed each other.

"I told you. Don't mention it." Cole's smile was crooked and endearing. "Besides. We went through something together. Something pretty enormous."

Whitney felt the same. She wanted to tell him that she had nowhere else in the world to be but right there in his family's home. She figured he already knew that.

Chapter Seventeen

The woman who sat in the passenger seat of Cole's pickup seemed nothing like the Whitney Silverton Cole had met in the Caribbean. She cupped her hands together as Cole drove off from the Remington House through the darkness, headed for the Katama Lodge.

On the radio, a DJ announced he planned to play twenty-four hours of ABBA. Cole snorted and said, "Does anyone need twenty-four hours of ABBA?"

Whitney's laugh came a little too late, proof that she hadn't been listening properly. Often throughout the day, she'd been like that— daydreamy and lost, especially within the chaos of Cole's family. More than once, Cole had worried that bringing Whitney to the Vineyard had been a mistake.

"Hey. Can I ask you a question?" Whitney asked suddenly. Her voice seemed very far away.

"Of course."

"Why did you leave those people behind?" Whitney

dropped her chin toward her chest as though the question had overwhelmed her.

Cole shook his head. "I asked myself that a lot when I was out to sea with a bunch of mean-spirited tourists."

"I can imagine. And then my idiotic ex-boyfriend showed you just how pure of heart the rest of the world really is."

"Maybe it was the punch I needed to wake me up from running away," Cole tried.

Whitney sniffed. A moment passed before she spoke.

"I've never told anyone this. When I was in my twenties, my dad met this woman, Liz. Eventually, they moved together to Miami, where he sold his boat and took on an entirely different life. I sailed for seven days to go visit him because I missed him desperately. At the time, I was partying a lot and felt very aimless. I couldn't believe he'd left me behind. I think he could see right through me. He pulled me aside and told me that he wished he hadn't had to run away his entire life. That always, he felt that the world was too much for him, and he had to keep a few steps ahead of it."

Cole's head pounded. He glanced toward Whitney, whose cheeks were glossy with tears. "What did you say to that?"

"I was angry," Whitney rasped. "So angry because it sounded to me that he belittled our life together. I'd loved our life. We'd had adventure after adventure. And now, here my father was, telling me that he hadn't fully enjoyed it the way I had. He'd stopped sailing around the world, but I had no intention to. I told him good luck with his boring life. And I headed out the door."

"Ooph." Cole winced.

"Yeah. That conversation is really heavy in my mind

right now for obvious reasons," Whitney breathed. "Especially because Garrett sort of said something similar when he left. That he just wanted somewhere or someone to come home to. I have no idea what that even looks like."

"Garrett is a—"

"I know. We don't need to spend another second insulting him," Whitney added. "I'm just saying. You know what it feels like to have a home. Don't squander that."

Cole's throat tightened. Slowly, he shifted his pickup across the front driveway of the Katama Lodge and hovered near the door. The temperature monitor in his truck told him it was forty-eight degrees. Whitney was probably freezing.

"Why don't you come out sailing with me tomorrow?" Cole said suddenly. "I got my boat out of storage, and I'd love to show you the Vineyard coastline. It's an entirely different world than the Caribbean. I think you'll love it."

Whitney turned to show enormous, hollow eyes. She looked like a scarecrow.

"I can't," she told him simply.

Cole dropped his shoulders forward. "Sometime this week, then? Seriously, I think you'll love it."

He wanted to guide her back to her one true love, sailing. He wanted to lift her spirits up any way he could.

"I'm sorry, Cole," Whitney told him. "You'll be the first to know when I'm ready. If I'm ever ready at all."

With that, Whitney shoved her weight into the passenger door and walked into the chill of the night. When she reached the front door of the Katama Lodge, she turned to give Cole a firm wave. She then flashed her key card over the door and slipped inside.

Cole remained in the purring truck for a good thirty

seconds. His limbs felt weak, and there was a subtle headache brewing in the back of his head. Whitney was a broken person; he could see that so clearly. He just hoped that his mother and the rest of the women at the Lodge could find a way to patch her back together again. He hoped that his friendship with Whitney would be the door through which she could find purpose for the rest of her life.

She couldn't go on like this.

Maybe she needed a home, no matter how many times she insisted she didn't.

Chapter Eighteen

Monday morning at six, Whitney entered Nancy's yoga studio with a rolled-up yoga mat under her arm. Other residents at the Katama Lodge already sat on their yoga mats with their hands placed gently near their knees and their faces serene. Nancy sat at the front, facing the yoga class. Her gray hair was vibrant and took in the light of the rising sun through the window. She looked like a lion.

Whitney grabbed a place in the back of the class and set up her yoga mat. She tried to model herself like the other women in the class, but the "serene" expression didn't suit her. It made her cheek tick.

Nancy greeted the class warmly yet quietly and instructed them to move into something called "Downward-Facing Dog." Whitney watched as the women moved their bodies delicately, leaning forward from their knees and placing their arms along the mat. Whitney tried the position but felt as though she flailed around awkwardly.

Sailing Home

"Focus on your breathing," Nancy instructed from the head of the class.

Whitney did as she was told at first. Inhale for four counts, then exhale for four counts. But on the third round, her mind started to pop and fizz with thoughts that weren't welcome. Images from her father's funeral tore through her. She yanked herself up from "Downward-Facing Dog" and gaped around the class. All of the women remained in that position, following blindly with whatever Nancy told them to do. *Was Whitney insane? Why was she putting herself through this?*

When the class returned to what Nancy called "Padmasana" (and what Whitney might have called "just sitting"), Whitney followed along as best as she could and forced her dark thoughts away. Each motion seemed overly silly and did nothing but give her mind space to think all of its most anxious thoughts.

Multiple times between the hours of six and seven, Whitney asked herself:

Why am I here? Why am I doing yoga?

Why am I in such a cold and gray place in the middle of the Atlantic?

Why did I listen to some twenty-eight-year-old kid's advice on how to live my life?

Why did Garrett leave me? Should I have married him when I had the chance, if only so I could say that I was married once?

The questions came hot and fast. Whitney clenched her eyes and willed them to stop, but they continued on. With every new yoga position, her brain presented more things to worry about. Each one seemed more urgent than the next.

Outside the yoga studio, Nancy approached Whitney to say hello.

"How was your first class?" Nancy asked. Apparently, she hadn't noticed how much Whitney had struggled.

"Oh! It was..." Whitney trailed off. *Was it better to lie in this situation?*

"Don't worry if you didn't take to it the first time," Nancy said. "It took me years to figure out what all this stuff was all about."

Whitney should have confessed right then and there that her mind and heart were in broken and jagged pieces, that she couldn't have done yoga properly if she'd actually tried. But instead, she just said, "I'm sure I'll get the hang of it. Thanks a lot for the class."

She had no idea how to ask for help.

Her first "real" day at the Lodge continued on much in the same way.

After breakfast, Whitney met with Janine, the actual Naturopathic Doctor. Janine greeted her warmly and professionally and said, "It was so lovely to have you at the Remington House over the weekend." She then proceeded to ask Whitney a series of questions about her stress levels, what she ate in a day, how often she slept, what her emotional triggers were, and what her current aches and pains were.

Here, Whitney could have told Janine just how brokenhearted she was.

But instead, she spoke about a weird "twinge" in her knee, which she'd had for years. She spoke about the "stress" of the accident down in the Caribbean, knowing that Janine already knew Cole's version. She avoided talking about her father, but she did mention that she'd hardly slept much the past few weeks.

Sailing Home

"I guess you could say I'm not feeling my best," Whitney offered finally, her eyes to the corner of the room.

She'd left out huge, gaping holes of information. Maybe she'd find the strength to fill Janine in on all of that during their next appointment. Or, maybe by then, she'd be gone.

"The thing about naturopathy," Janine began as their session closed, "is that we must trust in our body's ultimate wisdom. Your body already knows how to heal itself. It's up to you to listen to it."

Whitney wasn't sure what that meant. Instead of telling Janine that, however, she played along and said, "Absolutely! Makes sense to me." She then headed out the door and passed out in her room for a full two hours. *Where had this exhaustion come from? Was her depression getting worse now that she was on Martha's Vineyard? That went against the plan!*

That afternoon after lunch, Whitney attended her first "group talk." According to the Katama Lodge and Wellness Spa handbook, the group talk was essential to healing, as it allowed women from around the world to gather in empathy, discuss their struggles, and find ways to prepare one another for the next phase of life.

Whitney's group talk was made up of seven women. All of them were from off the island and had traveled to Martha's Vineyard exclusively for the Katama Lodge and Wellness Spa. They were between the ages of twenty-five and sixty-two and seemed overwhelmingly kind, so much so that Whitney felt like an alien compared to them. *Had she ever been "kind" like that before?* She wasn't sure she'd ever learned how.

The first woman who spoke was in her thirties. She'd

just had twins with her husband of two years, a guy named Mark. As she spoke about the sleepless nights, the crying babies, and her fears about being a mother, other women in the group spoke up to tell her that they'd often felt the same way during that first year of their children's development.

Whitney listened to these kind souls with an aching heart. She was the only one who had nothing to say. She'd hardly ever held a baby (although she'd often ached for one of her own, back when she and Garrett were really "happy").

The next woman was a bit older. Her exhaustion was linked to her sister, who had suffered a schizophrenic episode the previous year. "Since then, she's been living with me," the woman continued. "Her illness has affected everything in my life. It's kept me from doing the things I ordinarily do. And it's affected my marriage, as well. Believe me. I hate hearing myself say this. I love my sister to bits. It's just..."

"It's a lot," another woman at the meeting said. "And you're allowed to feel that way."

The other women at the meeting piped up, telling similar stories or else offering their support. Whitney remained quiet, stewing in her own thoughts.

She couldn't believe how broken this woman was. *Didn't she have a husband and a sister, both of whom loved her to bits? Didn't she have two people to come home to every single night?*

Whitney resented herself for these thoughts. She knew they were unfounded and that humans can break in all sorts of ways.

Still, when it came time for Whitney to speak about her own "damage," as it were, Whitney had no idea what to say. She couldn't tell these beautiful women, all of whom seemed to have families and loved ones and a million stories about their lives, that she was basically alone in the world. They couldn't relate to that at all. Maybe they would say something like, "Have you considered taking up a hobby to meet friends?" Or maybe they would say, "Oh, I met my husband on a dating app." She couldn't take it.

Whitney decided she wasn't eager to be judged by these women at all.

"I'm sorry," Whitney whispered, her voice rasping. "I um. I think I need a glass of water."

After that, she fled the room and didn't go back.

★ ★ ★

That night, Whitney couldn't sleep. Her phone seemed heavy with unread messages and emails, some from her lawyer, others from the guy who'd taken her boat into the warehouse, and a few from "friends" who'd learned about her "accident" and wanted to hear her side of the story.

Another message dinged in from Elsa, who'd apparently also heard that Whitney had left the "group talk" early.

> ELSA: I hope you're okay. Let me know if you want to talk one-on-one. I know that sometimes, group talk can be a lot for some people.

Whitney didn't answer. Instead, she shoved her feet into her tennis shoes, zipped up her sweatshirt, and wandered out into the inky darkness of the Katama grounds. Katama Bay sloshed across the sands, and

October winds rustled through the leaves. Their outline against the night sky was ominous and jagged.

Whitney wandered the grounds, her head so heavy that she had to tilt it downward. Beneath her, her feet hardly lifted from the ground. When she did reach the water, she removed her tennis shoes and socks and placed her feet on the icy chill of the sand.

On the other side of Katama Bay was Chappaquiddick Island, a name Whitney struggled to say aloud. On the other side of the bay, lights glinted, calling Chappaquiddick Island residents home. Whitney could remember long nights out at sea, during which she'd been the only human for miles and miles around. The only lights she'd known had been the stars in the sky.

Now, the idea of sailing from Martha's Vineyard to Chappaquiddick Island terrified her. The water seemed monstrously deep.

Her memories of the Great White Sharks off the coast of South America seemed like they belonged to someone else.

She was just a washed-up sailor, too frightened to return to the waters she'd once known. She would have to rewrite the story of her life. Maybe this was page one. Unfortunately, she had no idea what to write next.

Chapter Nineteen

"We're so glad you're back on the Vineyard." A voice rang out somewhere to Cole's left. He was bent low, securing the rope to the shifting sailboat he'd used for that late afternoon sailing lesson.

Cole turned to find the mother of the boy he'd just given a lesson to. The boy cowered behind his mother, so unlike the confident boy of twenty minutes ago. The one who'd said, "I finally know how to sail!"

"It's good to be back," Cole said, his voice wavering. He stood to full height and accepted seventy dollars, his going rate for a one-hour lesson. "And Billy's gotten a lot better. Haven't you, Billy?"

The mother waved a hand over Billy's head. Her voice lowered, she continued. "I heard you went through something pretty dramatic down in the Caribbean. I told my book club that you were my son's sailing instructor, and I promised them some gossip. What do you have for me?"

Cole's stomach twisted up. That wasn't a night he

liked to revisit. Besides, the version he'd given the people on the Vineyard wasn't entirely the "full version."

"I'm sorry to say I don't have gossip for you," Cole reported, although he didn't sound sorry in the slightest. "I wish I could help."

"Oh, come on." She dug into him, her eyes narrowing. "Everyone saw that big black eye."

"And everyone knows that I got that when the mast swung over and smashed into my eye," Cole countered. He then locked eyes with Billy to say, "Remember, Billy. I told you, always know where your mast is. It's super important. You got that?"

Billy and his disappointed mother disappeared down the dock and fell into the minivan parked nearby. Cole slung his backpack over his shoulders and headed back toward the boardwalk. A sunset played out like an impressionist painting to the west, and the air was warm for the second week in October. To Cole, this meant there was time for a beer at the local sailing bar just down the block.

To Cole's surprise, when he walked through the door of the rundown, pirate-themed sailing bar, he discovered his stepcousin, Alyssa, seated at the bar. She was in the midst of a heated argument with the bartender with the eyepatch.

"That's the thing," Alyssa stammered. "She's just a baby. But I swear, she knows what I'm thinking. My theory is that little kids can sense way more about adults than we give them credit for. Then slowly, as life wears us down, we lose that magical ability. What do you think?"

"I think I'd like to read a psychological study about that rather than listen to you blab tipsily at the local sailing bar," the bartender teased her right back. He then

Sailing Home

turned to find Cole and waved him over. "I have something for you to pick up. We need her out of here ASAP."

"Ha. Ha." Alyssa stuck out her tongue and then jumped up to give Cole a hug.

"I thought you were headed back to Brooklyn today," Cole said, genuinely pleased to see her.

"Maggie took Lucy back to Brooklyn to play 'mommy,'" Alyssa explained. "But I told Mom I'd help her with a few things around the house."

"Look at you. So domestic," Cole teased.

"Yeah, yeah." Alyssa rolled her eyes and sipped her beer. "Don't remind me that I've gotten boring over the past year. I already know."

"Sometimes, boring is healthy," the bartender reminded them as he poured Cole a pint. He then placed the drink in front of Cole and sped off to help a table in the corner.

Alyssa lifted her half-drunk glass to clink with Cole's. Her smile was mischievous. "Do you think he's right about that? That boring is healthy?"

Cole considered this. "I just had the most exciting few months of my life. I think I spent maybe twenty-five percent of that time genuinely happy. The other seventy-five percent of that time, I was miserable and lonely."

Alyssa wrinkled her nose. "I know what you mean. Like, when I took off for Spain last year with that horrible guy, I initially felt on top of the world. I was like, 'This is what freedom means!' But there was this deep and powerful feeling of loneliness and sorrow that fed that decision. I had to keep searching for something, anything if only to feel alive."

Cole still ached with sorrow for what had happened to Alyssa when she'd taken off with the guy from the

Netherlands to "see the world." She'd met that guy through Cole and Cole's island buds. In a way, he felt partially to blame.

"Don't you dare," Alyssa interjected.

"What?"

"Don't you dare apologize again," she said. "I told you. It was my own fault. I'll have to live with the consequences of that for the rest of my life."

Cole's shoulders dropped forward. He thought again of Whitney, of watching her faint onboard The Great Escape after getting everyone to shore safely.

"What do you think of Whitney?" Cole asked softly.

"Oh. She's..." Alyssa shook her head, surprised. "She's really quiet. Much quieter than I'd expected."

"Yeah. I think she's traumatized," Cole continued.

"Because of the accident? I mean, it wasn't anyone's fault," Alyssa countered.

"Yeah. It wasn't, in the version I told my mom," Cole shot back.

Alyssa's eyes glittered with intrigue. "You're holding out on me."

Cole then told her as much as he could remember. He explained meeting Whitney at the British Virgin Islands Regatta, her venomous ex-boyfriend, and Whitney's guilt about the way she'd reacted. This led to her asking Cole to be the "skipper" aboard her boat.

"But Whitney's dad was dying," Cole continued. "She didn't make it sound like it was all that bad yet. But one night, she told me that she would handle the course for the night. That I could relax. But that was the night she learned that her father had died. She lost all track of time and space. Meanwhile, upstairs, a fire broke out onboard. I

Sailing Home

managed to put it out quickly, but that was the moment we realized we were a whole lot closer to shore than we should have been. Whitney pulled out incredible strength to get us back to shore safely. But ever since that moment, she hasn't been on a sailboat. I'm not sure if she ever will again."

"Wow." Alyssa, who often knew just what to say, was speechless. "I mean. That's such terrible timing."

"The worst was that her ex-boyfriend was at the bar along the docks after we tied up. Whitney had fainted, and I was trying to get her to a hospital. I kept him from getting on the ambulance, and in return..."

"He gave you that black eye!" Alyssa cried, flabbergasted. "This is high-quality gossip, Cole. I can't believe you've kept this to yourself."

"Whitney's reputation has taken such a hit," Cole offered. "I just want to protect her. She's been through enough. And now..." He paused, trying to figure out how to continue. "Now, Mom tells me Whitney is having a hard time at the Lodge. It's already her second week there, and it sounds like she barely participates, attends only some of the classes, and doesn't pay attention to the guides they've given her. Mom isn't angry about it; she's just worried."

"I mean, that nutrition guide is not easy to follow," Alyssa pointed out.

Cole ignored her. "I can't help but feel guilty that I dragged her here with some stupid promise that she would 'get better.' What do I know?"

Alyssa tried to joke. "It's her fault for trusting you."

Cole rolled his eyes as Alyssa rebounded.

"I'm sorry. I'm obviously kidding. You're very trustworthy." She sipped her beer. "Cole, there's one thing I know. Only one. And it's this. Whitney, you, and I have all lost our fathers. Right?"

Cole nodded sadly.

"And each of us went through the trauma of that loss in very different ways," Alyssa continued. "Sure, my version of taking off for Spain wasn't the best version. But I'd argue there's no right way to handle loss. Maybe Whitney is taking this time to regroup. Maybe the Katama Lodge isn't perfect for her, but it gives her space and time alone."

"I guess you're right," Cole breathed.

"No, cousin. You know I'm right," Alyssa shot back, nudging him with her elbow. "Whitney knows she was lucky to meet you. She seems like one of the loneliest women I've ever met in my life. You've given her an anchor. You should be proud of that."

Chapter Twenty

It was mid-October already. Since her arrival at the Katama Lodge, Whitney had slowly morphed the clean-lined suite with its bleached sheets and white curtains into a sort of den or nest, where she hid from the outside world with packages of cookies and crackers. The television continually played sitcoms—many of which she'd seen Liz enjoy, which was funny to realize. She felt dead to the world. The worst of it was she hardly cared at all.

On top of it all, nobody had approached her about how infrequently she attended Lodge meetings and health sessions. She was content to limp through her days, avoiding all human contact until she felt it necessary to drop into a meeting or attend a class. When she did go, she hardly participated. *Why should she?* Very soon, she would have to figure out a way to build a new life elsewhere. Cole's family had graciously allowed her to stay, but it couldn't go on forever. Soon, they would forget about her. They would be happy when that time came.

Each night was the same. Her cheeks felt heavy from

snacking on salty foods, and her body was lethargic. Even still, she could not sleep. Once outside, she roamed the grounds, watched the water, and tried to remind herself of the woman she'd once been. *But who was that woman? Did she even make sense to Whitney any longer?*

One night, Whitney stood on the icy chill of the sand. She dared herself to wait until the water lapped across her toes. When she allowed it to happen, a shiver raced up her spine, and her brain seemed to open up and awaken. But when the water receded, it was like her soul, too, receded.

Where was she?

Suddenly, a voice rose from the darkness behind Whitney.

"Are you barefoot?"

Whitney whipped around to watch as Elsa appeared through the shadows, wrapped up like a burrito in a winter coat. Elsa's smile was warm and soft yet slightly guarded. Whitney had the sense that Elsa hadn't wanted to run into Whitney just then. She'd probably come down to the water at night for the same reason Whitney had. She wanted to be left alone.

But here they were— the woman who'd graciously allowed Whitney to stay at the Lodge alongside the woman who squandered that chance and wasted her days away.

Whitney realized she hadn't responded to Elsa's question. She swallowed the lump in her throat and scrambled around, hunting for her socks.

"Don't worry," Elsa told her as she removed her own shoes and socks. She winced at the sharp cold when she placed her feet on the sand. With tender and precise motions, she rolled her pant legs up her shins and stepped

Sailing Home

toward the slowly frothing water. "Cold water therapy is right in line with Katama Lodge principles, but I'm hardly ever brave enough to try."

Whitney dropped her sock and watched as Elsa stepped closer to the approaching water. Suddenly, Whitney felt herself jump to stand in line with Elsa. Their toes caught the light of the moon and seemed ghost-like across the sand. When the water draped across their toes and coated the tops of their feet, both Whitney and Elsa shrieked. This surprised Whitney a great deal. Normally, when she stood out there on the sand to touch the water, she emitted no sound.

But something about standing on the chilly sand with another person made the experience seem exponentially bigger yet easier to carry.

Why was that?

"Let's do it again," Elsa said excitedly as the water receded. "Wow. It feels like my entire brain is waking up. I should replace my cup of coffee with this every morning."

Whitney's smile felt unnatural. A pregnant silence filled the space between them. Slowly, Elsa's smile faded as well. The water lapped up again, but this time, neither of them made a peep.

"Whitney?" Elsa finally began, her eyes like saucers. "Why are you out here by yourself so late at night?"

Whitney swallowed. "I'd like to ask you the same question."

Elsa's chin wiggled, proof of her nerves. Whitney wondered if Elsa was just nervous about being around Whitney, especially because Whitney had closed herself off so successfully over the past two weeks.

"I don't know. It's hard to explain." Elsa placed her

hands over her eyes and took a deep, staggered breath. "And you'll probably think I'm crazy if I tell you."

Whitney thought that was laughable, although she kept it to herself. No one was crazier than Whitney. "Tell me."

"Sometimes, when I'm alone in my father's old office, I hear his voice," Elsa said, allowing her hands to drop to her sides. "The voice is always saying something simple— about repairs we need to make on the Katama Lodge, or how the guests are doing, or whether or not I need to take something to the bank. It's funny because I know the voice comes directly from my mind. But somehow, I hear it in his voice— and it takes me back to a few years ago when my father was my greatest ally and best friend. I never in a million years imagined my life without him. Yet now, here I am— edging toward my late forties. I'm engaged to a man who isn't my husband, and I'm basically in charge of the Katama Lodge. How did any of that happen?"

Whitney felt the sorrow peeking out from behind Elsa's smile.

"That's the question I keep asking myself, as well," Whitney breathed. "How did any of this happen?"

Elsa's eyes filled with tears and caught the light of the moon. Whitney had the sudden urge to throw herself into Elsa's arms and weep.

"I'm sorry that the Lodge isn't what you've needed it to be." Elsa's voice cracked.

"I—" Whitney hurried to explain herself, one way or the other. *But how?*

Instead, Elsa waved a hand. "Let me finish. Your time here at the Lodge has made me think back to my own time after my father's death. It was the heaviest depres-

Sailing Home

sion of my life. I hardly worked here at the Lodge and often considered throwing in the towel. I had no idea how to uphold my father's mission. It no longer made any sense to me.

"It's funny, thinking back on my father. He had this idea to build a lodge that would heal and restore women from all walks of life— women who'd stumbled somewhere along the way and needed a boost, a bit of support, a listening ear, and a helping hand. But as the Lodge became successful, our family life at home completely fell apart. It was ironic, wasn't it?

"When we were young, my brother, Colton, died in a freak horseback riding accident. Carmella always blamed herself for what happened. Unfortunately, our parents made it very difficult for her to think otherwise. I blame myself for that, as well. I should have been a more protective older sister. I should have put my foot down."

Whitney dropped her eyes to the sand. Shame was heavy across her shoulders. She wanted to say something about the selfishness of grief— that she'd spent the previous two weeks obsessed with her sorrow and believing nobody else could understand it.

"How do you keep going?" Whitney asked suddenly, surprised at how forward she sounded.

"Some days, I don't," Elsa answered honestly. "Some days, I look at the calendar, cancel all my plans, and walk along the water. Those days, I allow myself to think of my husband, my father, my brother, and my mother. I truly mourn them in everything I am and see them in everything around me. I see them in the water and the cliffside; I feel them in the fresh air. I know that to honor them well, I have to keep doing the best I can with the time I have left. God willing, I have a great deal of time left. But no one really knows, do they? So I take it one day at a time."

Whitney dropped down and wrapped her arms around her legs. She'd grown accustomed to the chill.

After a long pause, Whitney said, "Thank you for your honesty. I wish I knew how to be that honest about anything."

"It's taken me years to stare my own truth in the face," Elsa breathed. "Take all the time you need here at the Lodge. We're here for you if you need us. That's what my father wanted. It's up to me to carry out his dream."

Whitney's throat tightened with sorrow. "I wish I knew what my father wanted me to do. I don't think he wanted me to spend my life alone. But here I am, doing just that."

Elsa wrinkled her brow. "I can't pretend to understand what that feels like. But I hope you know that you don't have to be alone if you don't want to be. You're a remarkable person with a big and pure heart. You have so much to offer the world."

Whitney snorted. This definition was so different from the one she had for herself.

"I'm serious," Elsa spoke sharply. She tapped her finger to her temple. "At the end of the day, the only words we hear are the ones we tell ourselves. They have such power over us. I hope you learn to speak to yourself in a way that shows kindness and love. To me, it's the only way forward."

Elsa and Whitney held the silence for a long time, listening to the swell of the water across the bay. When the chill bit hard at their cheeks, they walked side by side back to the Lodge, heavy with personal sorrows.

Once in the foyer of the Lodge, Whitney scuffed her

shoes across the welcome mat. "I should probably check out soon. I've taken up too much of your time and space already."

But Elsa's eyes pleaded with her. "Give it a little more time, Whitney. At least till the end of October. There is so much sorrow in your eyes. I wouldn't feel right about sending you back out into the world. Not yet."

Chapter Twenty-One

Whitney hardly slept the rest of the night. By five fifteen, she'd spent hours tossing and turning her way across the bed, wrapping herself up in sheets and staring blankly at the light of the television. Sleep would not come for her. And so, at five thirty, she placed her toes delicately on the rug next to the bed, changed into a pair of yoga pants and a tank top, brewed a mug of tea, then headed out the door. She was third in line at the yoga studio, five minutes before Nancy arrived.

It wasn't that she wanted to be there. It was just that she'd seen something reflected in Elsa's eyes— an urgency that told Whitney that if she didn't give herself one final chance, maybe there would be no hope at all.

That week, Whitney pushed herself. She attended spa treatments, ate from the diet plan that Janine had drawn up for her, went to yoga classes, lay back as Carmella stuck her with acupuncture needles, and, sometimes, even got six or seven hours of sleep. She still stood out by the sand late at night, shivering as the waters erupted across her skin. "Cold water therapy" was apparently a thing she subscribed to, if nothing else.

The group sessions remained a struggle for Whitney. Since her arrival, the original women had been swapped out for other women— many of whom seemed on the brink of tragedy and devastation. Their stories about their divorces, loss of careers, painful fights with their children, or other such things were still difficult for Whitney to relate to. Sometimes, she opened her lips to tell her own story before closing them quickly and allowing someone else to speak. She couldn't trust anyone. She wasn't sure that would ever go away.

Toward the end of that week, Cole visited her in the Lodge cafeteria. They sat with green juices and watched an October rain patter across the big window. He told her about last year's hurricane, how it had torn across the island and destroyed anything in its way. Whitney had seen her fair share of tropical storms and hurricanes. Back then, she'd hardly been frightened of a little wind and rain, not even when she'd watched dramatic winds tear an entire bar from the ground and whip it across the beach. Her lack of fear had fascinated her. Now, all she felt was fear.

"Are you happy?" Whitney asked Cole as they walked toward the foyer, their juices drank and their conversation dried up.

"Most days," Cole told her. "And you?"

"I'm working on it," Whitney tried.

* * *

The next week, Whitney pushed herself to reach out to an old friend. Violet had been her dearest bud for years during the era when Whitney and Garrett had been inseparable. When Whitney had run into Violet at the British Virgin Islands Regatta, her heart had ballooned in her chest, reminding her of all the love she'd once had for that woman. *Was it too late to rekindle that friendship? Was it possible that Whitney was "worth" more than she thought she was— even after Garrett had left her behind?*

> WHITNEY: Hi, Violet. I'm sure this is coming out of left field, but I just wanted to reach out and say how wonderful it was to reconnect last month at the Regatta.
>
> WHITNEY: How are you and Hank doing? Congratulations again on your marriage.

Whitney stared down at the messages, imagining them flying out across the Atlantic and then the Caribbean Sea. Probably, Violet and Hank had just awoken on their sailboat, ready for a gorgeous day floating across turquoise waters. Probably, Whitney was the furthest thing from Violet's mind.

Still— they'd been friends. They'd once cared for one another deeply. Maybe this was a friendship Whitney could salvage. Perhaps she didn't have to be so alone.

The calendar on the wall told Whitney that she had two more days at the Lodge— one full day and a second half-day. It was now October 30th, just one day before Halloween, and the island outside her window was appropriately gloomy and slightly creepy. The branches on the trees had tossed off their leaves, and now, the branches and twigs were craggy against the gray morning sky.

Next, Whitney looked at flights. Her savings had remained untouched for the past month, which was a

Sailing Home

godsend. But she would soon need to make a whole lot more money, especially because the court case with Kenny Baldwin would begin sometime that winter— and the lawyer didn't exactly work for free.

The flights to the British Virgin Islands were reasonable. Whitney hovered her cursor over the BUY button but couldn't bring herself to click. The thought of returning to the sticky heat and the whispered questions about Whitney's "accident" didn't exactly thrill her. *But where on earth could she go?*

Whitney pushed off the decision till tomorrow. She knew that Elsa and the rest of the Lodge team had already rented her room out to another woman who planned to arrive on November 1st. This was Elsa's final countdown. After this, she would have to take care of herself alone.

That afternoon, Whitney sat in the group circle and watched as the other women walked in, most of them dressed in Katama Lodge robes, their hair hanging loosely across their shoulders or around their ears. Nobody bothered with things like makeup or curling irons, not at the Lodge. Elsa had told Whitney that this was a part of the Katama Lodge experience. Women were so tired of being judged in the outside world. It was healing to forget what you looked like for a little while.

Just before they were set to begin, Nancy entered the room with a big basket of Halloween candy. She wore a big witch's hat that drooped over one of her eyes and a fake mole, which she'd stuck on the side of her nose.

"Hello, everyone!" Nancy said. "I know we normally tout all things health here at the Lodge, but in my mind, a healthy lifestyle allows for a treat every now and again."

Each woman took one bite-sized candy bar. They lifted Reese's Cups, 3 Musketeers, Snickers, and

Butterfingers slowly, as though the sugar content might reach out from the packaging and bite them.

When the basket of candy reached Whitney, she stared into the basket and discovered, to her surprise, a single Baby Ruth bar. It was larger than the other bite-sized pieces in the basket and seemed to wink at Whitney knowingly.

For a long moment, Whitney gaped at the candy bar, awash with memories. How many times had her father leaped off their sailboat and headed straight for the local bodega, only to grab a beer for him and two Baby Ruths— one for him and one for her? Countless times. So much so that the taste of Baby Ruths was synonymous, for Whitney, with the feeling of watching the sunset after a long day at sea.

Whitney's eyes began to fill with tears. She was suddenly aware that all the women in the group session stared at her, aware that something was wrong. Whitney hadn't spoken once in the group session, not even in support of the other women. To the rest of them, she was a mystery. Maybe they didn't even like her.

"I'm sorry." Whitney's voice wavered as she reached into the basket and selected the Baby Ruth. Her hand shook. "I saw this candy bar and fell into silly childhood memories."

A woman across from Whitney— one who'd recently told a very sorrowful story about her brother's addiction problems and how they had affected her, piped up. "Childhood memories aren't silly at all. Sometimes, they're all we have."

The other women in the group nodded coaxingly, their eyes upon her. Whitney passed the basket of candy to the next woman and balanced the Baby Ruth on her

Sailing Home

knees. Instead of looking up at the woman, she continued to speak directly to the candy bar. Her nerves were insane.

"It was just my father and me for so long. My mother never wanted to be a mother and was never in the picture. That never mattered to us. We sailed everywhere— across the Caribbean, down and up the coast of South America, all the way to Maine, and across the Atlantic Ocean. Together, we met thousands of other sailors, taught ourselves three different languages, and made up so many card games that we often mixed up the rules and got into silly fights about them."

The women in the room were captivated by Whitney's stories.

"You basically grew up on a sailboat?" one of the women asked, genuinely shocked.

"Yeah." Whitney sniffed. "My dad never saw any reason to have a home. He said the world was our home. Well, until he met Liz."

"Uh-oh," another woman said under her breath. "I've never met a kind woman named Liz."

Whitney laughed in spite of herself. "That isn't fair to all Liz-es," she said. "But this one is a trip. She gave my father a home in Miami, and he never looked back. I felt abandoned somehow. Like he'd taught me how to live a certain way, and I didn't know any other way. I wandered through the rest of my twenties, sailing and meeting people who weren't exactly nice to me. And then, out of nowhere, I met a man named Garrett."

The women were rapt with attention. Whitney stuttered as she continued to describe her love for Garrett and the life they'd built together. She then explained the cracks in the relationship and how, on one fateful day, she'd discovered he was cheating on her.

"After ten years of traveling the world together?" one woman in the group demanded.

Whitney nodded. She was hovering on the brink of tears. "I just felt so stupid. Suddenly, I'd lost my father and my boyfriend. My career was at a new high, but emotionally, I was at a new low. I limped through the next few years, going from race to race. Suddenly, my father died of lung cancer, and I made the biggest mistakes of my career. It's the kind of mistake you can't really come back from."

A woman across the room shook her head. "Honey, you can come back from any mistake."

"I don't know," Whitney offered.

"We've all done terrible things," another woman breathed.

"It's part of the reason we're here," another said.

Another woman with jet-black hair was close to tears. "I wrecked my car with my baby son in the back seat. He was in the hospital for six weeks. That was seven years ago. He's healthy and happy, the star of his soccer team. But I can't get over this guilt."

Whitney's heart cracked at the edges. Before she could speak, another woman chimed in.

"My brother's addictions made me hate him," she said. "I screamed at him once that I wished he would just leave me alone. After that, he..." She trailed off, overwhelmed.

The mood in the room shifted. Everyone suddenly seemed on the same page. Whitney recognized just how incorrect she'd been about these women. They were here to connect, not to judge. They saw themselves in her

Sailing Home

story, too. It was up to her to hold up their stories as well, to fall into the empathy of their connections. It was up to her to help them rebuild, just as they helped her.

"Where's Garrett now?" the woman beside Whitney asked, arching her brow.

Whitney's heart lifted. "I'm not sure. And for the first time in a very long time, I don't care where he is or what he does. I hope I never see him again. But if I do, I hope he sees me as the woman I become— a stronger woman who holds all the stories of my past yet makes room for the stories of my future."

"It's all we can do," another woman whispered.

Whitney blinked back tears and tore at the wrapper around the Baby Ruth. Her eyes closed while she took a tentative bite. As the chocolate melted across her tongue, waves of nostalgia poured over her. For the first time in a long time, she was able to sit in it without shoving it away. Maybe this was the first step.

When Whitney returned to her room that night, she received a message from Violet.

> VIOLET: Omg, it's you! I loved seeing you at the Regatta last month, but I have to admit that seeing you made me feel so guilty. I know I should have reached out to you more after Garrett did what he did. That is on me. I was a terrible friend.
>
> VIOLET: Are you doing okay, sweetie? I've heard a few things, namely that you left the islands. Are you back? Can we meet?

> VIOLET: I don't want you to be alone right now. I can't imagine what you're going through. But we can get through this together. Just say the word, and I'll meet you wherever you want to go.

Whitney held the phone to her chest and swayed from side to side, her heart softening. The world could be a terribly cruel place. But love was always there if you opened yourself up to finding it.

Chapter Twenty-Two

"Hey there." The following afternoon, Elsa appeared in the doorway of her office, removed her reading glasses, and smiled at Whitney. Both knew it was Whitney's final moments at the Lodge. It had been a crazy month.

Whitney bundled up in her newly purchased jacket and scarf, her backpack strapped to her back. The cold was nothing she would ever understand— but she could finally breathe again.

"Hey." Whitney smiled.

"I wanted to make sure I caught you before you left," Elsa said. "Where did you decide you're off to?"

Whitney's stomach twisted with anxiety. "I wish I could tell you."

"It's a secret?" Elsa asked, her eyes widening.

"Nope. I just still haven't decided." Whitney laughed, at a loss. "My only plan right now is to meet up with Cole at his bar near the Yacht Club."

"Oh, that dirty old place." Elsa looked mischievous.

"My husband dragged me there all the time. The pirate theme is a bit much."

Whitney laughed. "I can't wait to see it." After a pause, she stepped up toward Elsa and hugged her gently.

"You're going to get through this," Elsa whispered.

Whitney decided not to fight her on that. It had to be true. It just had to be.

When Whitney turned back, she paused at the door and spoke mostly to the wall. "Meeting Cole at the Regatta genuinely changed my life. I hope you know that you have a very special son. If I had ever become a mother, I would have hoped for a son half as kind as he is."

Behind Whitney, Elsa whispered, "Thank you for saying that. I'm sure your father felt the same about you."

Whitney grabbed an Uber and headed to the Edgartown Yacht Club. After several weeks of full-on Katama Lodge life, she was grateful to see other sights. She cracked the window in the back seat so that chilly air sliced across her cheek. The driver of the Uber said, "Happy Halloween!" as she got out of the car. When Whitney glanced back, she realized the driver was dressed as Indiana Jones. She wished him a happy holiday back.

The bar where most sailors hung out was directly next to the Edgartown Yacht Club, decorated with pirate decorations, an explosion of fake spiderwebs, ghoulish masks on the wall, ghosts hanging from the ceiling, and scary movies playing on each of the TVs. Whitney laughed to herself and sat at the bar to order a beer from the bartender, who had an eye patch. It wasn't clear if the eye patch was for medical purposes or just a costume. Regardless, the eye patch suited him.

As she sipped her beer, she assessed the other patrons at the bar. A middle-aged couple dressed as Edward Scissorhands and his lover, Kim, ate through a large basket of wings and occasionally eyed one another with love in their eyes. Two older sailing types drank pints and chatted about the good old days. Others either drank alone or glanced at the door, waiting for someone.

Whitney's phone buzzed.

> COLE: Hey. I'm sorry, I'm running a little late. It's a long story.

> WHITNEY: Don't worry! I have no schedule. Free as a bird, as they say.

Free as a bird, yes. Potentially too free. Whitney scrambled to search on her phone for nearby hotels or inns. Several of them had already closed for the season. She glanced up to ask the bartender his top cheap hotel or motel recommendations. He said that cheap was difficult to come by in Martha's Vineyard.

Whitney checked on the ferry times to leave the island. If she had a couple of drinks with Cole and then headed back to Oak Bluffs to grab the ferry, she could get on a bus and head somewhere else. Somewhere with a cheap motel and enough internet access so that she could research where to go next. It seemed insane to go more inland; she'd hardly ever bothered with that kind of travel. Was there something good about the open road? Maybe she could go see.

Whitney sipped her beer and wandered toward the jukebox in the corner. The CDs inside presented a wide array of genres— everything from rock to R&B to pop and beyond. Led Zeppelin, Papa Roach, Aaliyah, Pink!, The Killers— countless familiar artists, passed her by.

And then suddenly, Whitney stumbled on a piece of musical gold.

"Come Sail Away" by Styx had been her father's favorite song. It was truly epic, with everything from an iconic piano solo to angels that turned out to be aliens. The lyrics were killer, as well, saying, "I look at the sea. Reflections in the waves spark my memory. Some happy, some sad. I think of childhood friends and the dreams we had."

Memories of her father singing that song made her heart ache. She reached for her wallet, on the hunt for a dollar bill. Unfortunately, she had nothing but a few pennies and her debit and credit cards. This was a cashless society, but the jukebox seemed not to care.

"Excuse me? Do you need a dollar?" A man's voice came from a few tables to the right of the corner jukebox.

Whitney turned swiftly to find a handsome man with a mass of wild hair around his ears and a healthy tan. He looked to be in his mid-forties, maybe. His eyes seemed to swallow her, although the soft light of the bar shadowed the rest of his face.

"Oh, it's not a big deal," Whitney said. It actually was, but she wouldn't tell a stranger that.

"Come on." The man stood and stepped around his table, removing his wallet. A dollar flashed out of his wallet. It was suddenly in Whitney's hand.

"Oh." Whitney sniffed and said, "Thank you." She then fed the jukebox the dollar and selected her song.

The opening piano solo plinked through the speakers.

Sailing Home

The man sighed and laughed. "Styx, huh? A classic. I don't think I've heard it in years."

Whitney continued to stare ahead, growing lost in the music. When the lyrics began, she heard herself begin to sing. "I'm sailing away. Set an open course for the virgin sea. 'Cause I've got to be free. Free to face the life that's ahead of me."

To her surprise, the man who'd given her the dollar sang along with her. His voice was clear with a slight vibrato. Whitney turned to look at him, really look at him. Something in her gut leaped with a sense of familiarity. But she hadn't met him before. *Had she?*

"Wait a minute," the man said suddenly, arching one of his thick eyebrows. "Aren't you Whitney Silverton?"

Ordinarily, Whitney detested this question. This time, however, she let it float past her.

"No. I'm not," she returned. "Are you Whitney Silverton?"

At this, the man threw his head back with laughter so that his dark hair danced in the light. His laughter was nourishing and alive.

"I'm not Whitney Silverton, no," he said. "Although I truly wish I was. She's one of the best sailors alive."

Whitney smirked. "Aren't you clever?"

The man shrugged. "I like to think I have a bit of brain between these two ears."

Whitney assessed him. She knew him. *Didn't she?* It was on the tip of her tongue. But suddenly, the Styx song burst into its wild finish, surging from a ballad to an all-out rock tune. Both she and this man sang through the end, dancing in front of the jukebox as the other people at the bar looked on.

Whitney hadn't lost herself in music like that in years.

It felt like a religious experience, as though she'd given herself over to a higher power.

After that, the music cut out. The man eyed her and said, "You know, one dollar gets you three songs."

"I guess it's your turn, then," Whitney said.

"Hmm." The man tapped his lips and approached the jukebox. Whitney headed back to the bar to order herself another round. The air simmered with expectation.

As the bartender poured Whitney a second beer, the first bars of "Brandy (You're A Fine Girl)" buzzed through the speakers. Whitney eyed the handsome stranger and pounded the bar.

"You've got to be kidding me," she said.

"What?" The man danced his way back to the bar as he sang the first bars. "There's a port on a western bay, and it serves a hundred ships a day. Lonely sailors pass the time away and talk about their homes…"

"Yeah, yeah." Whitney rolled her eyes. "Sounds like my entire life."

The man opened his lips, preparing to speak. He was no more than five inches away from her; Whitney's body felt terribly aware of that. Her skin felt like it was on fire.

"Hey!" Cole popped up on the other side of Whitney, bouncing onto a stool at the bar. "Sorry, I'm late."

"Ah!" Whitney greeted Cole with a hug and beckoned back toward the stranger. "This is…"

"Rowan." The man's smile widened, showing the intensity of his white teeth. He shook Cole's hand, his brow furrowing.

"Wait." With the mention of his name, Whitney's memory clicked. "Rowan." She clapped a hand over his bicep with surprise. Unsurprisingly, that bicep was thick

Sailing Home

and powerful— the sort of thing that could pick her up easily.

Rowan nodded knowingly.

"At the Regatta..." Whitney whispered.

"The British Virgin Islands Regatta?" Cole asked.

"We met briefly," Rowan said of Whitney. "Through friends of friends. Although in the sailing community, everyone seems to be a friend of a friend."

"Gosh..." Whitney continued to gape at him, that handsome man from that fateful day. It had been September 10th, fewer than two months before. The stunning warmth and the glorious waters and the vibrant sailors all seemed a part of someone else's memories now.

"And you," Rowan continued, "must be Aiden Steel's son. You're the spitting image of him. I've read about you on the circuit. A real up-and-comer."

Cole gaped at Rowan in genuine disbelief. "How could you have been in the British Virgin Islands and also know my father?"

Rowan ruffled his hair. "I grew up on Nantucket. Your dad and I used to get into loads of trouble back in the day. Racing up and down the Nantucket Sound as if our lives depended on it. I tried my darnedest to get him to go down to the Caribbean with me, but unfortunately for me, he was much too in love for anything like that."

Cole's eyes glittered with tears. Whitney turned her eyes from Rowan to Cole and back again, overwhelmed at the intensity of this moment. She'd been locked away at the Katama Lodge for weeks. *Was this what the real world was actually like?*

"Brandy (You're A Fine Girl)" petered out after that, leaving the bar in heavy silence.

"What a small world," Rowan said finally, eyeing Whitney knowingly.

Whitney punched Rowan lightly on the bicep. "You knew I was Whitney Silverton all along."

"Yes, well. You didn't seem to know it was you," Rowan pointed out. "And I've been wrong before."

"Have you?" Whitney giggled and sipped her beer.

It was hard to believe that this friend of a friend had grown up with Cole's father. Over the next twenty minutes, Rowan spoke at length about Aiden Steel and the hilarity of their early days together. Cole's eyes continued to widen.

"I've never heard these stories," Cole said finally, his shoulders drooping. "And to be honest, I always wondered if my dad regretted not going somewhere else to really pursue sailing."

To this, Rowan shook his head wildly so that his hair ruffled around his ears. "I didn't see your dad that much over the years, but we managed a beer now and again when I popped up to Nantucket to see my folks. Each time, all he did was brag about his three children and his wife. It was enough to drive me crazy, actually. Not because I didn't like hearing about you. I did. But because I worried that I'd made the wrong decision."

Rowan held the silence for a moment, his eyes growing shadowed. "I never got married or had any children. I was never allowed to teach my children the great tradition of sailing. Know that your father saw you as the greatest gift of his life, Cole. He never regretted it for a minute."

Cole was clearly overwhelmed. He sipped his beer without speaking, looking out across the bar without seeing anything at all. The bartender with the eye patch reminded them that they had another song to play on the jukebox, but none of them stood up to tend to it.

Eventually, Rowan stood up to head to the bathroom. In the quiet of that moment, Whitney placed her hand on Cole's shoulder and said, "I'm sorry. I had no idea he knew your father."

Cole shook his head. "I love those stories. They keep him alive a little bit longer."

"I can understand that."

Cole pressed his lips together. He looked genuinely exhausted, his cheeks hollowed out and his skin pale. Whitney wanted to ask him what was wrong.

But instead, Cole asked her, "Where are you headed after this?"

Whitney shrugged. "I'll probably head back to the mainland and stay in a motel. Maybe after that, I'll fly back to the British Virgin Islands to grab my boat."

"You don't have to leave," Cole piped up. "Winters here are cozy and quiet. Maybe that's what you need?"

Whitney's lips parted with surprise. She hadn't expected this idea.

"I mean, you could stay in a cheap apartment. Come over for family dinners. Drink at this bar. Get into the nitty-gritty of Martha's Vineyard winters."

Whitney hesitated. "Maybe," she whispered. "I'll really think about it."

Cole nodded. He pressed the back of his hand against his eye and sniffed back tears. "I think I might have to get out of here," he said after he finished the last of his first beer. "I don't know what's gotten into me. I guess it's just the weather."

Whitney stood and hugged Cole close. To her, he was the little brother she'd never had, the mentee that had changed her perspective of the world, and a friend with more kindness in his little finger than most people had in their entire body.

She would see him again. She just wasn't sure when or how.

Chapter Twenty-Three

Back in his pickup, Cole bent his head over the steering wheel and forced himself to breathe. He'd had only one beer, so his abilities were completely intact. His heart, however, seemed to burst against his rib cage, threatening to tear all the way through him.

"Come on, Cole. Pull yourself together." He sniffed and rubbed at his nose, started the engine, and pulled out from the sailing bar parking lot. Somewhere back behind him, Whitney and Rowan drank on— chasing after the chaos of the night.

Meanwhile, Cole had bigger fish to fry.

Cole parked outside his apartment complex. Jitters rolled through him, making his fingers tap-tap across his thigh and his feet smack against the brake pedal. His apartment window showed only the soft light from the television. *What the heck would he do now?*

Cole walked like a zombie toward the back staircase that led to his second-story apartment. Each step brought him closer to his doom. His head was bulbous and heavy from the stories that Rowan had told him. Rowan's friendship with Cole's father had really put a wrench in things that night. Cole hadn't needed another level to his emotional baggage. He'd already gone through enough.

Outside his door, Cole reached for his key before remembering that he'd left it behind. He only had one. It had been needed here with her.

Cole rapped the door and waited, his shoulders hunched, defeated. "It's me," he called, loud enough for her to hear. After another pause of nothingness, he knocked on the door a final time.

Suddenly, the door lurched open to reveal his little stowaway.

Aria stood in a pair of pajama pants and a light pink sweater. Her blond hair curled out in all directions, and her eyes were half open and sleepy. She was like a dream woman Cole had concocted in the back alleys of his mind. Someone he would have longed to come home to.

The only thing was— he didn't want anything to do with Aria. She'd appeared out of the blue that afternoon as he'd stepped off his sailboat. *"Please, Cole. Can we talk?"* He'd told her it would have to wait, that he had plans with a friend— a friend who planned to leave the island for good.

He'd driven Aria home, left her there, and wandered through the rest of the night, stewing in anxiety. *What on earth could she possibly want? And why had she traveled all the way to Martha's Vineyard to see him?* He'd already begun to extricate her from his memories. The Baldwin family had just been the turning point of the rest of his life – proof that he didn't want anything to do with the ritzy high-class families who glommed onto the sailing community.

Sailing Home

None of it added up.

But it was time to face the music. Here she was, looking at him the way she always had, as though he was the only man in the world. Cole couldn't remember a single woman who'd ever looked at him like that.

"You're back." Aria sounded breathless. She beckoned for him to enter and shut the door behind him.

Cole took stock of his apartment. In the hour since he'd left her there, she'd washed the dishes and the countertops, vacuumed the carpeting, dusted the television, and thrown out the moldy fruit from the bowl on the table. The air was fresh, smelling of lavender. How had she done that?

"Oh. Wow." Cole palmed the back of his neck, at a loss for what to say. Slowly, he knelt into a kitchen chair and gestured toward the one across from him. Aria sat and folded her hands in front of her on the table. For a moment, they simply regarded one another— there in the closet-sized kitchen of Cole's temporary apartment.

Cole was vaguely sure Aria had never been in an apartment so scummy before.

"Aria?" Cole shook his head, aghast. "Can you tell me what you're doing here?"

Aria dropped her eyes to the table. Little half-moons lingered beneath her eyes, proof that she was tired. She was a different creature than the free-spirited woman he'd met aboard *The Great Escape*. He supposed that he was, too.

"I convinced my father to drop the lawsuit against Whitney," Aria breathed.

Cole was surprised. Whitney had mentioned the lawsuit a few times in passing, always with a vague resignation. Kenny Baldwin didn't seem like the type to let up.

"That whole trip was cursed," Aria continued. "I don't know what I was thinking when I agreed to go on it in the first place. But I told my father that I researched more about Whitney. That she just lost her father. That she's clearly not in a good place right now."

"And he accepted that?" Cole was doubtful.

"No." Aria chuckled. "But I did tell him that if he didn't drop the lawsuit, I would find a way to disappear from his life and never come back."

Cole's jaw dropped. This was a story he hadn't anticipated. "What did he say?"

"He freaked out, of course. Said I was manipulating him. But then, I told him something I've thought about for a long time. That I actually don't want a relationship wherein manipulation is the key tactic. I want a father-daughter relationship— without money or necessity."

Cole tilted his head. "That means you..."

"I don't have any monetary ties to my father," Aria finished. "For the first time in my life, I'm out here alone in the world. Just like everyone else."

Cole was genuinely speechless. He'd imagined Aria to be a rich girl, through and through. The kind who talked badly about their father but always ran to him when times got tough.

"We signed official paperwork on it and everything," Aria said, waving her hands. "After that, I downloaded something called LinkedIn to look for jobs. Do you have any idea what that is?"

"Vaguely." Cole's smile was crooked. *Who was this woman? Why was she so infectious?*

"Anyway." Aria's cheeks were blotchy with embar-

Sailing Home

rassment. "You'd said you were on Martha's Vineyard. I just wanted to come here and tell you in person that I'm sorry about everything that happened."

"You could have written me on social media," Cole pointed out.

"No." Aria heaved a sigh. "No, because it's so much bigger than that. I've spent the past month dreaming about you. I wanted to come here and, I don't know. Take a chance. With you."

Cole thought this girl had seen one too many romantic comedies. He held his breath, taking in the beauty of this moment before he shattered it.

And then he said, "Aria, we don't know each other."

Aria seemed unfazed. After a dramatic pause, she said, "I understand that. But listen, Cole. I feel like I've dated every son of every rich man across the world. They're all the same. Arrogant. Overbearing. Obsessed with cryptocurrency. Ugh."

Cole laughed in spite of himself.

"Let's just go out on one date," Aria suggested. "One little ice cream sundae at the local diner, or whatever people do on dates in small towns."

"That's about right, actually," Cole joked.

Aria's laughter filled the little kitchen. The air around them was like a bubble on the verge of popping. Cole eventually joined her laughter, although he wasn't entirely sure what was so funny.

"I'm going to finally stand on my own," Aria said suddenly, dabbing the corners of her eyes with the end of her sleeve. "Finally going to see the world on my own terms and not from the window of a private jet. I can't tell you what it feels like, having this freedom for the first time."

"It sounds terrifying," Cole tried.

Aria's eyes glittered with tears. "Yes. But anything worthwhile is terrifying, isn't it?"

Cole's heart lifted. In the silence, they studied one another. At twenty-eight and twenty-four, they had the rest of their lives stretched out before them, unwritten. *Would they find space for one another in those stories? Or was this just a blip on the way to something else?* There was no telling.

"Oh." Aria snapped her fingers suddenly, breaking the reverie. "I wanted to ask you."

"Sure. Go ahead."

"Do you know anyone who's hiring? Rent was always other people's problem. Now..."

"Welcome to the real world, Aria," Cole said. He then pondered for a moment, remembering a NOW HIRING sign in the front window of the very diner she'd just picked fun at. "I hope you like ice cream sundaes a whole lot. Because you might just be in luck."

Chapter Twenty-Four

Rowan opened his wallet as wide as it could go, turned it over, and shook it. "Nope. Not a single dollar bill in sight."
Whitney collapsed against the jukebox and wailed with laughter. The very last song they'd selected on the jukebox continued to jangle out ABBA's "Gimme Gimme Gimme."

"I can't believe that was the last one we chose," she said sadly as the last chords petered out.

"Our judgment is not the best right now," Rowan agreed, his smile enormous.

Back at the bar, the bartender with the eye patch scrubbed the top of the bar and eyed them with his one eye. "You know that closing time was fifteen minutes ago, don't you?"

Whitney and Rowan locked eyes and burst into another round of reckless giggles. In every sense, Whitney felt like a wild-eyed teenager on the brink of the rest of her life. There was no way she was forty-three and deep in the biggest depression spiral of her life. There was just no way.

"Where did the time go?" Rowan asked.

"I'd like to know," Whitney shot back.

Rowan grabbed his debit card, insisting on paying for the last two rounds. Whitney was very used to telling other sailors that they couldn't buy her drinks; it was strange, then, to relinquish control and watch his debit card fly through the reader. His signature on the receipt was authoritative and easy.

She felt safe with him. Safe in a way she couldn't fully name.

Back outside, a sharp Halloween wind rattled through their bones. Whitney screeched and fell against Rowan, who spontaneously wrapped his arms around her and held her until the sharp wind passed. When it did, Whitney laughed and stepped away from him, wide-eyed. Along the water directly beside them, docks surged and were lined with several sailboats, which creaked gently in what was left of the wind.

"What time is it?" Whitney had forgotten to check back at the bar.

"It's eleven-twenty," Rowan recited. He swept his hand through his hair and zipped his jacket the rest of the way to his chin. "And if I'm not mistaken, we're thousands and thousands of miles away from the Caribbean, where we should be."

"Ha." Whitney's cheeks burned with a mix of chill and embarrassment. "I don't know if I can ever go back there."

Rowan tilted his head. "That's ridiculous, Whitney. It's your home, isn't it?"

"I'm not sure if I ever knew what that meant," she breathed.

Another horrible wind ripped through them. Whitney wrapped her own arms around herself and huddled in a ball. Rowan's grin widened. He liked her—really liked her. It wasn't just fascination with who Whitney Silverton might have been; it was real.

"Where are you headed tonight?" he asked suddenly. "I wouldn't be a gentleman if I didn't walk you home."

Whitney realized with a funny jolt that she'd forgotten to continue researching nearby hotels. "Oh. Shoot."

"You didn't book a place?" Rowan asked.

"Urgh. It's a long story. I've been sort of off the grid the past month or so," Whitney continued. Her eyes smarted as she added, "Since the whole thing with my dad and the accident happened."

She didn't have to ask him to know he'd already heard all the gossip there was to hear. He was a part of the tight-knit sailing community and had assuredly heard it all. Despite that, he'd still stuck around this long, hanging with her deep into the night. That said something.

Where could she go? Maybe she could walk the streets of Edgartown and amble into one hotel or another? She would probably have to pay upward of three hundred dollars.

"Why don't you come sleep on my boat?" Rowan said suddenly.

Whitney's eyes widened. Fear swept through her. This was the first man who'd asked her to "come home with him" since Garrett. But besides that, Whitney hardly knew him.

"I know. I know." He waved his hands between them.

"I wouldn't have asked if it didn't seem to be an emergency. But listen. I have a large berth for separate sleeping. I have two very thick sleeping bags for warmth. We'll be at least ten feet from one another, with no direct view of each other. You can pretend I'm not there."

His eyes were so kind and open, reflecting the light of the moon.

"I..." Whitney began to protest. *How could she tell him that she hadn't been onboard a sailboat since the accident? How could she tell him that she was now deathly afraid of the water?*

But suddenly, Rowan placed his hand between them. "I'll make you coffee in the morning, and from there, you can plan your next adventure. What a privilege to be a part of Whitney Silverton's pit stop between epic stories."

He was infectious. Whitney closed her eyes against the tornado of emotion, placed her hand in his, and allowed him to guide her back to his boat.

Once in the warmth of the berth, Rowan set up her sleeping bag, showed her where everything was, and turned out the light. In only a few minutes, over ten feet away, Rowan's breathing pattern changed. He drifted into a deep sleep.

This left Whitney alone in the darkness. Above her bunk, a large window stretched over her, through which she could see a splendorous smattering of stars. She now felt in tune with all the other versions of herself who had fallen asleep beneath similar blankets of stars. She'd been a part of the world and all its mysticisms.

Beneath her, the sailboat rocked her gently, to-and-fro in the waters of Katama Bay. Like a child, she drifted into the soft nothingness. There were no nightmares awaiting

Sailing Home

her, only sweet dreams of wide-open waters and laughter and sun.

* * *

The next morning, Rowan and Whitney feasted on eggs, jam on toast, and several mugs of instant coffee. Even after the perfectly planned meals at the Katama Lodge and Wellness Spa, Whitney felt that this breakfast was especially nourishing for her in both body and soul.

Sunlight danced across the water. When they spoke, their breath steamed with the November 1st chill. Often, Whitney and Rowan locked eyes at length, lost in one another's beauty. When he asked her what her plans were for the next part of her life— she told him she still hoped to make it up as she went along.

After breakfast, Whitney packed her backpack and stepped off the boat. The boat shifted slightly beneath her, a reminder of the tenuousness of water. This time, the fear didn't latch to her at all.

"Oh! I think I might need that phone number, now," Rowan said, rubbing the back of his neck nervously as he passed over his phone.

"Right." Whitney bit her lower lip as she typed out her number and returned it.

"I hope you won't be a stranger," he told her.

"I'm sure we'll run into each other at one Regatta or another," Whitney said.

"Yeah. The great Whitney Silverton, back to the races."

Rowan's smile seemed rather sad. The air was heavy with the weight of their goodbye. Finally, Whitney stepped forward, threw her arms around him, closed her eyes, and allowed herself to be held. Really held.

"Thank you. For everything." She whispered it, although she knew he probably couldn't possibly understand.

Whitney then stepped out of the hug, turned on a heel, and hustled toward the boardwalk. November wind rattled through her ears. When she reached the boardwalk, she turned back and watched as, already, Rowan sailed out toward the Edgartown Lighthouse. His sails fluttered, catching the light of the sun like a butterfly's wing.

Whitney's eyes welled with tears. "Don't you dare," she muttered to herself, drawing to her full height. "You're Whitney Silverton. And you don't..."

Sunlight flashed across a sign, which hung on the outer edge of a nearby sailboat. The sign said: **"FOR RENT - CALL 555-6755. LONG-TERM RENTALS."**

Whitney gaped at the sign. It seemed somehow metaphorical, a perfect ticket out of the gray darkness of the north and back into the glorious turquoise of her forever home. Perhaps she'd been overthinking this "home" stuff, anyhow. Perhaps the Caribbean had always been that for her; she'd just been too naive to lend herself to multiple definitions of "home."

Just as Whitney reached for her phone to call the long-term rental company, a text buzzed through.

> UNKNOWN NUMBER: Let's meet next week.

Sailing Home

> UNKNOWN NUMBER: Somewhere where the sun shines, and the wind is fresh and good.

Whitney closed her eyes. Hope swelled through her, rising swiftly like the tide. She could feel Rowan's heart somewhere out there on the open seas. It waited for her.

Coming next in the Katama Bay Series

Pre – Order A Sister's Blessing

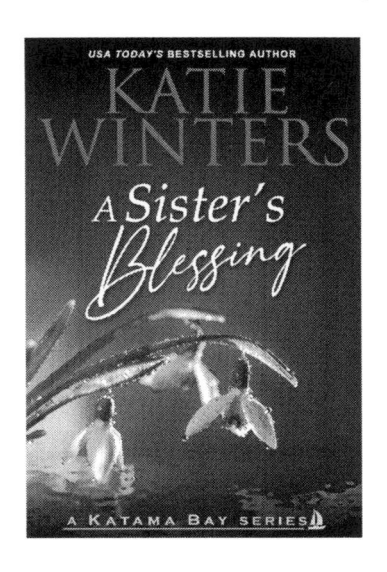

Other Books by Katie

The Vineyard Sunset Series
Sisters of Edgartown Series
Secrets of Mackinac Island Series
A Katama Bay Series
A Mount Desert Island Series
A Nantucket Sunset Series